"I just can't imagine under what circumstances you think I'd ever, ever, even consider marrying *you*."

His gaze didn't flicker. "How about the one when I agree to save your business?"

She stared at him, the shock of his words making the edges of her vision turn watery.

"Save my business—" she repeated slowly.

He nodded. "If you agree to become my wife." He paused, studying her face. "It's up to you, or of course—" he was speaking with a mock courtesy that made her want to hurl her bag at his head "—I can just leave. The choice is yours."

Her skin was prickling, and her heart was beating so loudly that it was getting in the way of her thoughts.

"That's not a choice," she said hoarsely. "That's blackmail."

For what felt like a lifetime, he stared at her thoughtfully, and then finally he gave a casual shrug.

"Yes, I suppose it is. But on some level all business is blackmail."

His face was impassive, his eyes steady on hers.

"And that's what this is, Margot. It's just business."

Louise Fuller was a tomboy who hated pink and always wanted to be the prince—not the princess! Now she enjoys creating heroines who aren't pretty pushovers but are strong, believable women. Before writing for Harlequin she studied literature and philosophy at university, and then worked as a reporter on her local newspaper. She lives in Tunbridge Wells with her impossibly handsome husband, Patrick, and their six children.

Books by Louise Fuller

Harlequin Presents

A Deal Sealed by Passion
Claiming His Wedding Night
Blackmailed Down the Aisle
Surrender to the Ruthless Billionaire

Visit the Author Profile page
at Harlequin.com for more titles.

Louise Fuller

REVENGE AT THE ALTAR

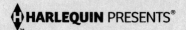

⬧ HARLEQUIN PRESENTS®

Recycling programs
for this product may
not exist in your area.

ISBN-13: 978-1-335-50484-5

Revenge at the Altar

First North American publication 2018

Copyright © 2018 by Louise Fuller

This is a work of fiction. Names, characters, places and incidents are either the product of the author's imagination or are used fictitiously, and any resemblance to actual persons, living or dead, business establishments, events or locales is entirely coincidental.

This edition published by arrangement with Harlequin Books S.A.

For questions and comments about the quality of this book, please contact us at CustomerService@Harlequin.com.

HARLEQUIN®
www.Harlequin.com

Printed in U.S.A.

REVENGE AT THE ALTAR

To the Nell, for holding my hand on the plane,
and not cutting your hair!

All my love.

CHAPTER ONE

As the wheels of her private jet hit the runway Margot Duvernay looked up from her laptop and gazed pensively out of the window, her fingers twisting at the 'Team Bride' wristband on her arm.

As CEO of the legendary House of Duvernay champagne business, she worked hard. The last five years had been particularly challenging, both emotionally and financially—so much so that, incredibly, Gisele's bachelorette week in Monte Carlo was the first time off she'd had in months.

But her father Emile's unexpected message had abruptly cut short her stay.

Walking purposefully across the T tarmac, she climbed into the waiting air-conditioned limousine and pulled out her phone. She replayed his message, frowning at the giggling and the Bossa Nova music she could hear in the background. If only she had picked it up sooner, she thought regretfully, her soft brown eyes creasing. Emile was just so unreliable, and so easily distracted…

But on the plus side he had definitely mentioned *selling* his shares, and that was a first.

Leaning back against the seat, she watched as the beautiful mansard-roofed headquarters of her family's two-hundred-and-fifty-year-old business came into view, feeling a familiar mix of pride and responsibility. She loved everything about the building—the cool, quiet interior, the sense of history in the wood-panelled boardroom and the symmetry of the façade. To her, it was more than just bricks and plaster. It was a legacy—and also a burden.

Just like the position of CEO.

Margot breathed out slowly.

Growing up, she had never imagined being in charge of Duvernay—never once wanted the power or the responsibility. By nature, she loathed being in the spotlight, and after graduating she'd been happy to head up the company's newly created environmental department.

However, her older brother Yves's tragic death on the ski slopes of Verbier had left her with no alternative but to take over the family business. Of course, Emile would have liked the status of running a global brand. But even if he hadn't been cold-shouldered by his in-laws, he preferred topping up his tan to analyzing market trends. Her brother Louis might have been taller than her, but at just sixteen he had been far too young to step up, and her grandfather had been too old, too devastated by grief. It had been hard enough for him to deal with his daughter's accidental drug overdose, but the shock of losing his grandson too had caused a series of strokes from which he had still not fully recovered.

And so it had been left to Margot to do what she had always done—pick up the pieces—and that was why she was hurrying back to Epernay this morning.

Inside the brightly lit foyer, the reassuring familiarity of everything calmed her slightly, but as she stepped into the lift her phone began to vibrate in her hand and she felt her composure wobble. Glancing down at the screen, she drew in a quick, shaky breath and her heart began to pound with a mixture of hope and relief.

Thank goodness! Finally it was her father.

'Emile. I was just about to call you—'

'Really? I thought you might be sulking.'

Gritting her teeth, Margot felt a spasm of irritation. Honestly, her father was so exasperating, and so monumentally thoughtless sometimes. When he hadn't returned her messages she had started to panic, to worry that maybe he'd changed his mind. Clearly, though, he'd just been playing hard to get.

But now she could hear the elation in his voice and suddenly she didn't care about his stupid games. What mattered was that she knew he'd been telling the truth. Finally he was ready to sell the shares.

Her heart began to beat faster.

The timing couldn't be better.

Not only would it mean that the business would be whole again in time for her brother Louis's wedding, it would also give her grandfather a much-needed boost. Since his last stroke he hadn't been himself, but this would be the perfect tonic. For this wedding was more than just a romantic ceremony—it was about continuing the family name and ensuring the future of Duvernay.

She felt her chest tighten. And, of course, for her, buying back her father's shares would have an additional and thankfully undisclosed benefit of sending a strong message to the bank.

'Oh, Papa.' Her father was such a child, but today of all days she was prepared to indulge him, and so, despite her annoyance, she spoke placatingly. 'You know I've been trying to get hold of you. I must have rung you at least a dozen times.'

She felt a rush of excitement as she played

back her father's rambling message inside her head. He'd mentioned something about flying up to Reims, but that had been hours ago. She glanced at her watch. Surely he must be here by now?

Her mouth was suddenly almost too dry to get words out. 'Where are you staying? I can come to you, or I can send a car to pick you up.'

Her pulse accelerated. She couldn't believe it. Finally it was happening. The moment she'd been waiting for almost her whole life.

Buying back the 'lost' shares, as her grandfather referred to them, was a goal that had preoccupied her since she'd taken over the reins of the business. In doing so, she would not only make Duvernay whole again, she would also bring closure to the whole sorry complex mess of her parents' marriage and the repercussions that had followed her mother's tragic death.

She felt her pulse tremble.

Her father and her grandparents had always had a fraught relationship. Emile might look like a film star, but to them he was just a horse trainer—eloping with their nineteen-year-old daughter had not endeared him to her straitlaced and image-conscious family. His decision to live off Colette's trust fund had merely deepened the rift.

But after her death, it had been his refusal

to turn over her shares to his children that had turned a difficult relationship into a bitter stand-off.

Emile had always claimed it was an act of self-preservation. Her grandparents had seen it as an act of spite. Either way, the facts were undeniable. Her father had threatened to take her and her brothers to Switzerland if he wasn't allowed to hold on to the shares, and her grandfather had agreed to his demands on two conditions: that he give up custody of his children to his in-laws and that they keep their mother's name.

Margot shivered. Once she had thought that grief might bring the two sides of her family closer. In fact the reverse had happened. There was still such bad blood between Emile and his in-laws that even now they both took every opportunity to point-score.

But maybe now that might finally change.

The thought made her heart leap upwards. It would just be so wonderful to put all of this behind them before Louis's wedding. Her first task, though, was to pin Emile down…

'Papa?' she repeated, trying to sound casual. 'Just tell me where you'd like to meet.'

'That's why I'm calling—'

His voice had changed. He sounded a little uneasy—defiant, almost—and briefly she wondered why. But before she had a chance to give it any more thought he started talking again.

'I did try, so you can't blame me— Not now, *chérie*, put it over there. I waited as long as I could…'

Hearing a soft but unmistakably feminine murmur, Margot frowned. Even now her father couldn't manage to give her his full and undivided attention. Her mouth thinned. No doubt he was already celebrating the upcoming sale of his shares with his current batch of hangers-on.

And then her heartbeat froze, and she felt her fingers tighten involuntarily around the phone as his words bumped into one another inside her head like dodgems at the funfair. 'Blame you for what?'

'I waited as long as I could, *poussin*, but it was such a good offer—'

His use of her childhood nickname as much as his wheedling tone sent a ripple of alarm over her skin. Her father only ever called her *poussin*—little chick—when he wanted something or when he wanted to be forgiven.

'What offer?' she said slowly.

The lift doors opened and she stepped out into the glass-ceilinged atrium. Straight ahead, she noticed her PA hovering nervously in front of her office door, and her heart gave a sickening thump.

'What have you done, Papa?

'I've done what I should have done a long time ago.' The wheedling tone had shifted, become defensive. 'So I hope you're not going to make a fuss, Margot. I mean, it's what you've been telling me to do for years—sell my shares. And now I have. And I have to say I got a damn good price for them too.'

It was as if a bomb had exploded inside her head. Blood was roaring in her ears and the floor seemed to ripple beneath her feet.

'You said that if you were going to sell your shares you'd come to me first.' Margot felt panic, hot and slippery, run down her spine.

'And I did.' There was a burst of laughter in the background and she felt her father's attention shift and divert away from her. 'But you didn't pick up.'

'I couldn't. I was having a massage.' She let out a breath. 'Look, Papa, we can sort this out. Just don't sign anything, okay? Just stay where you are and I will come to you.'

'It's too late now. I signed the paperwork first thing this morning. And I *mean* first thing. He got me out of bed,' he grumbled. 'Anyway, there's no point in getting out of shape with me—just talk to *him*. He should be there by now.'

'Who—?' she began, but even without the tell-tale clink of ice against glass she could tell her father was no longer listening.

She heard the click of his lighter, then the slow expulsion of smoke. 'Apparently that's why it all had to be done so early. He wanted to get up to Epernay…take a look around headquarters.'

Margot gazed dazedly across the honey-coloured parquet floor. No wonder her staff were looking so confused. Clearly the newest Duvernay shareholder was already on site. But who was he—and what had he told them?

Her pulse stuttered in time with her footsteps. There were already enough rumours circulating around the company as it was—and what would the bank think if they heard that Emile had suddenly decided to sell his shares?

Silently she cursed herself for not picking up her messages—and her father for being so utterly, irredeemably selfish.

'It'll be fine,' Emile was saying briskly.

Now that the worst was over he was clearly itching to be gone.

'You're so rational and practical, *poussin*.'

She could almost see him shuddering even at the concept of such qualities.

'Just talk to him. Maybe you can persuade him to sell them back to you.'

He was desperate to be off. If Margot had been the sort to scream or hurl abuse she would have unleashed the tide of invective churning in her throat. But she wasn't. A lifetime of watching the soap opera that had been her parents' marriage had cured her of any desire for a scene. For a moment, though, she considered telling Emile in the most *ir*rational, *im*practical terms exactly what she thought of him.

Only, really, what was the point? Her father's 'me first' morality was precisely why he'd kept the shares in the first place.

'Although somehow I doubt it…'

Her father exhaled again, and she pictured him stubbing out his cigarette with the same careless force with which he had upended her dreams of taking back control of Duvernay.

'He seemed absolutely set on having them. But, truthfully, I think I might have done you a favour. I mean, he *is* the man of the moment, right?'

The man of the moment.

Margot blinked. Her brain was whirling, her thoughts flying in a hundred directions. She had read that headline. Not the article, for that would have been too painful. But, walking through the centre of Paris last month, she had found it impossible to tear her gaze away from the newsstands. Or more particularly the head-and-shoulders shot that had accompanied the article, and those eyes—one blue, one green—staring down the Champs-élysées as if he owned it.

'Man of the moment?'

Her voice sounded blurred, shapeless—like a candle flame that had burnt the whole wick and was floundering in wax.

'Yeah—Max Montigny. They say he can turn water into wine, so I guess he'll give those stuffy vignerons a run for their money— Yeah, I'll be right there.'

Margot tried to speak, but her breath was thick and tangled in her throat. 'Papa—' she began, but it was too late. He was talking over her.

'Look, call me later—well, maybe not later, but whenever. I love you, but I have to go—'

The phone went dead.

But not as dead as she felt.

Max Montigny.

It had been almost ten years since she'd last seen him. Ten years of trying to pretend their relationship, his lies, her heartbreak, that none of it had happened. And she'd done a pretty good job, she thought dully.

Of course it had helped that only Yves had ever known the full story. To everyone else Max had been at first a trusted employee, and later a favoured friend of the family.

To her, though, he had been a fantasy made flesh. With smooth dark hair, a profile so pure it looked as though it had been cut with a knife, and a lean, muscular body that hummed with energy, he had been like a dark star that seemed to tug at all her five senses whenever she was within his orbit.

Only as far as he was concerned Margot had been invisible. No, maybe not invisible. He *had* noticed her, but only in the same jokey way that her own brother had—smiling at her off-hand-edly as he joined the family for dinner, or casu-ally offering to drive her into town when it was raining.

And then one day, instead of looking through her, he had stared at her so intently she had for-gotten to breathe, forgotten to look away.

Remembering that moment, the impossibility of not holding his gaze, her cheeks felt suddenly as though they were on fire.

She had been captivated by him, enthralled and enchanted. She would have followed him blindly into darkness, and in a way she had— for she had gone into his arms and to his bed, given herself to him willingly, eagerly.

From then on he had been everything to her. Her man of the moment. Her man for ever.

Until the day he'd broken her heart and walked out of her life without so much as a flicker of remorse in those haunting eyes.

Afterwards, the pain had been unbearable.

Feigning illness, she'd stayed in bed for days, curled up small and still beneath her duvet, chest aching with anguish, throat tight with tears she hadn't allowed herself to weep for fear that her grandfather would notice.

But now was not the time for tears either and, swallowing the hard shard of misery in her throat, Margot greeted her PA with what she hoped was a reasonable approximation of her usual composure.

'Good morning, Simone.'

'Good morning, *madame*.' Simone hesitated. Colour was creeping over her cheekbones and she seemed flustered. 'I'm sorry, I didn't know you were coming in today. But he—Mr Montigny, I mean—he said you were expecting him.'

Smiling, Margot nodded. So it was true. Just for a moment she had hoped—wanted to believe that she had somehow misunderstood Emile. But this was confirmation. Max was here.

'I hope that's okay…?'

Her PA's voice trailed off and Margot felt her own cheekbones start to ache with the effort of smiling. Poor Simone! Her normally poised PA looked flushed and jumpy. But then no doubt she'd been a recent recipient of the famous but sadly superficial Montigny charm.

'Yes, it's fine, Simone. And it's my fault—I should have called ahead. Is he in my office?'

She felt a stab of anger. Max had only been back in her life for a matter of minutes and already she was lying for him.

Simone shook her head, her confusion giving way to obvious relief. 'No, he said that he would like to see the boardroom. I didn't think it would be a problem…'

Margot kept smiling but she felt a sudden savage urge to cry, to rage against the injustice and cruelty of it all. If only she could be like any other normal young woman, like Gisele and her friends, drinking cocktails and flirting with waiters.

But crying and raging was not the Duvernay way—or at least, not in public—and instead she merely nodded again. 'It's not. In fact, I'll go and give him the full guided tour myself.'

Straight out the door and out of my life, she thought savagely.

Turning, she walked towards the boardroom, her eyes fixed on the polished brass door handle. If only she could just keep on walking. Only what would be the point? Max Montigny wasn't here by chance. Nor was he just going to give up and disappear. Like it or not, the only way she was going to turn him back into being nothing more than a painful memory was by confronting him.

And, lifting her chin, she turned the door handle and stepped into the boardroom.

She saw him immediately, and although she had expected to feel *something*, nothing could have prepared her for the rush of despair and regret that swept over her.

It was nearly ten years since he had walked out of her life. Ten years was a long time, and everyone said that time was a great healer. But if that was true why, then, was her body trembling? And why did her heart feel like a lead weight?

Surely he shouldn't matter to her any more? But, seeing him again, she felt the same reaction she had that first time, aged just nineteen. That he couldn't be real. That no actual living man could be so unutterably beautiful. It wasn't possible or fair.

He was facing away from her, slumped in one of the leather armchairs that were arranged around the long oval table, his long legs sprawled negligently in front of him, seemingly admiring the view from the window.

Her heart was racing, but her legs and arms seemed to have stopped working. Gazing at the back of his head, at the smooth dark hair that she had so loved to caress, she thought she might throw up.

How could this be happening? she thought dully. But that was the wrong question. What she needed to ask—*and answer*—was how could

she *stop* it happening? How could she get him
out of her boardroom and out of her life?

Letting out a breath, she closed the door and
watched, mesmerised, as slowly he swung round
in the chair to face her. She stared at him in silence. This was the man who had not only broken her heart, but shattered her pride and her
romantic ideals. Once she had loved him. And
afterwards she had hated him.

Only clearly her feelings weren't that simple—or maybe she had just forgotten how effortlessly Max could throw her off balance. For
although heat was rising up inside her, she knew
that it wasn't the arid heat of loathing but something that felt a lot like desire.

Her mouth was suddenly dry, and her heart
was beating so fast and so loud that it sounded
like a drumroll—as though Max was the winner in some game show. She breathed in sharply.
But what was his prize?

Gazing into his eyes—those incredible het-
erochromatic eyes—she saw herself reflected
in the blue and green, no longer nineteen, but
still dazzled and dazed.

All those years ago he had been model-hand-
some, turning heads as easily as he now turned
grapes into wine and wine into profit. His
straight, patrician jaw and high cheekbones had
hinted at a breathtaking adult beauty to come,

and that promise had been more than met. A shiver ran through her body. Met, and enhanced by a dark grey suit that seemed purposely designed to draw her gaze to the spectacular body that she knew lay beneath.

Her breath caught in her chest and, petrified that the expression on her face might reveal her thoughts, she pushed aside the unsettling image of a naked Max and forced herself to meet his gaze.

He smiled, and the line of his mouth arrowed through her skin.

'Margot...it's been a long time.'

As he spoke she felt a tingling shock. His voice hadn't changed, and that wasn't fair, for—like his eyes—it was utterly distinctive, and made even the dullest of words sound like spring water. It was just so soft, sexy...

And utterly untrustworthy, she reminded herself irritably. Having been on the receiving end of it, she knew from first-hand experience that the softness was like spun sugar—a clever trick designed to seduce, and to gift-wrap the parcel of lies that came out of his mouth.

'Not long enough,' she said coolly.

Ignoring the heat snaking over her skin, she stalked to the opposite end of the room and dropped her bag on the table. 'Why don't you give it another decade—or two, even?'

He seemed unmoved by her rudeness—or maybe, judging by the slight up-curve to his mouth, a little amused. 'I'm sorry you feel like that. Given the change in our relationship—'

'We don't *have* a relationship,' she snapped.

They never had. It was one of the facts that she'd forced herself to accept over the years—that, no matter how physically close they'd been, Max was a cipher to her. In love, and blindsided by how beautiful, how alive he'd made her feel in bed, she hadn't noticed that there had been none of the prerequisites for a happy, healthy relationship—honesty, openness, trust...

The truth was that she'd never really known him at all. He, though, had clearly found *her* embarrassingly easy to read. Unsurprisingly! She'd been that most clichéd of adolescents: a clueless teenager infatuated with her brother's best friend. And, of course, her family was not just famous but *in*famous.

Even now, the thought of her being so transparently smitten made her cringe.

'We don't have a relationship,' she repeated. 'And a signature on a piece of paper isn't about to change that.'

His gaze held hers, and a mocking smile tugged at his mouth as he rotated the chair back and forth.

'Really?' He spoke mildly, as though they

were discussing the possibility of rain. 'Why don't we call my lawyer? Or yours? See if they agree with that statement.'

Her head snapped up. It was a bonus that Max hadn't spoken to Pierre yet, but the very fact that he was hinting at the possibility of doing so made her throat tighten.

'That won't be necessary. This matter is between you and me.'

'But I thought you said we didn't have any relationship?'

She glared at him, hearing and hating the goading note in his voice.

'We don't. And we won't. I meant that this matter is private, and I intend to keep it that way.'

Max stared coldly across the table. Did she *really* think that he was going to let that happen? That she was in control of this situation.

Nearly a decade ago he had been, if not happy, then willing to keep their relationship under wraps. She had told him she needed time. That she needed to find the right moment to tell her family the truth. And he had let her beauty and her desirability blind him to the real truth—that he was a secret she would never be willing to share.

But he wasn't about to let history repeat itself. 'Are you sure about that? I mean, you know

what they say about good intentions, Margot,'
he said softly. 'Do you really want to head down
that particular road?'

There was a taut, quivering silence, and Margot felt her face drain of colour, felt her body, her
heart, shrinking away from his threat.

There's no need! she wanted to shout into his
handsome face. *You've already cast me out of
heaven and into a hell of your making.*

But she wasn't going to give him the satisfaction of knowing how raw her wounds still were
and how much he had mattered to her.

She returned his gaze coldly. 'Are you threat-
ening me?'

Watching the flush of colour spread over her
collarbone, Max tilted his head backwards, savouring her fury. He had never seen her angry
before—in fact he'd never seen her express any
strong emotion.

At least not outside the bedroom.

His pulse twitched and a memory stole into
his head of that first time in his room—how the
directness of her gaze had held him captive as
she had pressed her body against his, her fingers
cutting into his back, her breath warm against
his mouth.

Margot might have been serious and serene
on the surface, but the first time he had kissed
her properly had been a revelation. She'd been

so passionate and unfettered. In fact, it had been not so much a revelation as a revolution—all heat and hunger and urgency.

Suddenly he was vibrating with a hunger of his own, and he felt heat break out on his skin. Slowly, he slid his hands over the armrests of the chair to stop himself from reaching out and pulling her against him. The muscles in his jaw tensed and he gritted his teeth.

'Only the weak and the incompetent resort to threats. I'm merely making conversation.' He looked straight into her flushed face. 'You remember conversation, don't you, Margot? It's the thing you used to interrupt by dragging me to bed.'

Margot stared at him, her body pulsing with equal parts longing and loathing. If only she could throw his words back in his face. But it was true. Her desire for him had been frantic and inexorable.

She lifted her chin. So what if it had? Enjoying sex wasn't a crime. And it certainly wasn't sneaky or dishonest—like, say, deliberately setting out to seduce someone for their money.

Eyes narrowing, she yanked out one of the chairs with uncharacteristic roughness and sat down on it. Pulling her bag closer, she reached inside.

Max watched in silence as she pulled out a

fountain pen and a leather-bound case. Ignoring him, she flipped it open and began writing with swift, sure strokes. Then, laying the pen down, she tore the paper she'd been writing on free and pushed it across the table towards him.

It was a cheque.

A cheque!

His breathing jerked and his jaw felt suddenly as though it was hewn from basalt. He didn't move, didn't even lower his gaze, just kept his eyes locked on her face as with effort he held on to the fast-fraying threads of his temper.

'What's that?' he asked softly.

Her mouth thinned. 'I don't know how your mind works, Max, and I don't want to, but I know why you're here. It's the same reason you were here ten years ago. *Money.*' Margot gestured towards the cheque. 'So why don't you just take it and go?'

He was watching her thoughtfully, his expression somewhere between incredulous and mocking. But there was a tension in him that hadn't been there before.

'That's amazing,' he said finally. 'I didn't know people actually did this kind of thing in real life. I thought it was just in films—'

'If only this was a film,' she said coldly. 'Then I could just leave you on the cutting room floor.'

Max gazed across the room, anger shrinking

his focus so that all he could see was the small rectangular piece of paper lying on the tabletop. Of course it would come down to money. That was all their relationship had ever been about. Or, more precisely, his complete and utter lack of it.

Margot was a Duvernay, and Duvernays didn't marry poor outsiders. His breath seemed to harden in his lungs. Not even when they had claimed them as family, welcomed them into their home and their lives.

Briefly he let the pain and anger of his memories seep through his veins. Officially he might have been just on the payroll, but for nearly three years he had been treated like a member of the clan—and, stupid idiot that he was, he had actually come to believe in the fiction that although blood made you related, it was loyalty that made you family.

Later, when his perception hadn't been blunted by desire and emotion, it had been easy to see that any invitation into the inner sanctum had been on their terms, and it had never extended to marrying the daughter of the house.

Only by then he had lost his job, his home and his pride. He had been left penniless and powerless.

But times had changed. Leaning back, he smiled coldly. 'It's not enough.'

Margot clenched her jaw, her brown eyes glowing with anger like peat on a fire. 'Oh, believe me, it is.'

Even if she had written a row of zeros it would be more than he deserved. He had already cost her enough—no, too much—in pain and regret.

'So take it and go.'

He shifted in his seat, and she felt another stab of anger that he should be able to do this to her. That after everything he'd already taken he could just swan back into her life, into her boardroom, and demand more.

Controlling her emotions, she closed her chequebook with exaggerated care and looked up at him. 'Why are you here, Max?'

He shrugged. 'Isn't that obvious? I'm a shareholder and a director now, so I thought we should talk.'

'You could have just telephoned,' she snapped.

'What?' His mouth curved up at one corner. 'And miss all the fun.' He let his eyes home in on the pulse beating at the base of her throat. 'Besides, I wanted to choose my office.'

She watched almost hypnotised as he gestured lazily around the room. 'Pick out a desk…wallpaper maybe…'

Folding her arms to stop her hands shaking, she glowered at him. The shock of everything—her father's phone message, Max buying the shares, his sudden and unwelcome reappearance in her life—was suddenly too much to endure a moment longer.

'Just stop it, okay? *Stop it*. This is insane. You can't seriously expect to work here. Or want to.'

He raised an eyebrow. 'Is there a problem?'

She looked at him in disbelief. 'Yes, of course there's a problem. You and me…our history—'

Breaking off, she fought to control the sudden jab of pain at the memory of just how cruelly one-sided that history had been.

'I don't care how many shares you buy, you are not stepping foot in this boardroom again. So how much is it?' She forced a business-like tone into her voice. 'How much do you want?'

She waited for his reply but it didn't come. And then, as the silence seemed to stretch beyond all normal limits, she felt her spine stiffen with horror as slowly he shook his head.

'I don't want and I certainly don't need your money.'

Watching the doubt and confusion in her eyes, he felt suddenly immensely satisfied. Buying the shares had been an act of insanity on so many levels, but now, having Margot in front of him, knowing that his mere presence had dragged her here, it all felt worth it.

Colour was spreading slowly over her cheeks. 'Take the cheque or don't—I don't care.' She lifted her chin. 'But either way this conversation is over. And now I suggest you leave before I have you removed—'

'That's not going to happen.' His voice sounded normal—pleasant, even—but she felt a shiver of apprehension, for there was a strand of steel running through every syllable that matched the combative glint in his eyes.

'I'm not just the hired help now, baby. I'm CEO of a global wine business. More importantly, as of today, I'm a bona fide director of this company.'

He paused, and she felt as if the air was being sucked out of the room as he let his gaze linger on her face. Pulse racing, she realised that only a very foolish woman would underestimate a man like Max Montigny.

'*Your* company.'

He lounged back, and suddenly her heart was thumping against her ribs.

'Although that may be about to change.'

'What do you mean?' Her voice was like a whisper. She cleared her throat. 'What are you talking about?'

He shrugged. 'Right now you might live in the big chateau, have a private jet and a chauffeur-driven limousine, but I've seen your accounts.'

She frowned, started to object, but he simply smiled and she fell silent, for there was something knowing in the gaze that was making her skin start to prickle with fear and apprehension.

'Your father showed them to me. And they make pretty bleak reading. Desperate, in fact. Oh, it all looks good on the outside, but you're haemorrhaging money.'

Margot could feel the colour draining from her face. His words were detonating inside her head like grenades. Suddenly she was deaf, dazed, reeling blindly through the dust and rubble of the mess she had sought so hard to contain, struggling to breathe.

'That's not true,' she said hoarsely. Her lungs felt as though they were being squeezed in a vice. 'We've just had a difficult few months—

'More like five years.' He stared at her for a long moment, his gaze impassive. 'You asked me why I'm here. Well, that's it. That's why. Your family is about to be ruined and I want to be here to see it.'

He stared at her steadily, his eyes straight and unblinking, and Margot stared back at him, stilled, almost mesmerised by his words. 'What are you talking about?'

'I'm talking about retribution. You and your family ruined my life, and now I get to watch your world implode.'

Margot shook her head. Stiffening her shoulders, she forced herself to look him in the eye.

'No, you seduced me, and then you asked me to marry you just so you could get your hands on my money.'

For a moment he didn't reply, then he shrugged, and it was that offhand gesture—the casual dismissal of the way he'd broken her heart—that told her more clearly than any words that he was being serious.

Watching the light fade from Margot's eyes, Max told himself he didn't care. She deserved everything that was coming. They all did.

'And I paid for that. You and your family made sure I lost everything. I couldn't even get a reference. No vineyard would touch me.'

Remembering the shock and helplessness he'd felt in the hours and days following Margot's rejection, he bit down hard, using the pain of the past to block out her pale, stunned face.

'Now it's your turn.'

He leaned back against the leather upholstery, his eyes never leaving hers.

'I only bought shares in your company to get a ringside seat.'

CHAPTER TWO

MARGOT SAT FROZEN, mute with shock, her heart lurching inside her chest like a ship at sea in a storm.

'How dare you?' Blood was drumming in her ears, and her body vibrated with anger and disbelief. 'How dare you stand here in my boardroom and—?'

'Easily.'

She watched in mute horror as Max stood up and, raising his arms above his head, stretched his shoulders and neck. His apparent serenity only exacerbated the anxiety that was hammering against her ribcage.

'And I'll find it easier still to stand in your office and watch the administrators repossess that beautiful custom-made Parnian desk of yours.'

He was walking towards her now, and suddenly her breath was coming thick and fast.

'That won't happen.' She stood up hastily, her

gaze locking on his, trying to ignore both the intense maleness of his lean, muscular body and the way her pulse was jumping like a stranded fish in response to it.

'Oh, it will.'

He stopped in front of her, his eyes—those beautiful hypnotic eyes—pinning her to the floor even as her head spun faster.

'Your business is in a mess, baby—a bloated, unstable, debt-ridden mess. House of Duvernay?' His eyes narrowed. 'More like house of straw!'

'And you're the wolf, are you? Come to huff and puff?' she sneered, her gaze colliding with his.

It was the wrong thing to say—not least because there was more than a hint of the wolf about his intense, hostile focus and the restrained power of body. For a moment, she held her breath. But then he smiled—only it felt more as if he was baring his teeth.

'I won't need to.' He studied her face. 'I won't need to do anything except sit back and watch while everything you love and care about slips through your fingers.'

The air was vibrating between them. 'You're a monster,' she whispered, inching backwards. 'A cold-blooded barbarian. What kind of man would say something like that?'

He shrugged, his expression somewhere between a challenge and a taunt. 'The kind that believes in karma.'

Margot was struggling to speak. She wanted to deny his claims. Prove him wrong. But the trouble was that she knew that he was right.

The business *was* a mess.

Her brother Yves might have resented his glamorous parents, but he had been more like Colette and Emile than he'd cared to admit, and five years after his death she was still trying to clear up the consequences of his impulsive and imprudent management style. Only nothing she did seemed to work.

Her heart began to beat faster. How could it? She didn't have her great-grandfather's vision, or her grandfather's ruthless determination and drive. Nor was she full of Yves's flamboyant self-assurance. In fact, if anything, the opposite was true. She'd found the responsibility of ensuring that the family legacy stayed intact increasingly overwhelming and as her self-doubts grew the profits continued to shrink. Finally—reluctantly—she'd decided to put up the chateau as security.

Her pulse began to beat faster.

Even just thinking about it made her feel physically sick. Not only had the chateau belonged to her family for sixteen generations, in less than two months it was supposed to be the setting for her brother Louis's wedding.

It had been a last-ditch attempt to reassure the bank. Only it hadn't worked. Max was right. The business was failing.

She shivered.

Or rather *she* had failed, and soon the whole world would know the truth that she had so desperately tried to hide.

Watching her in silence, Max breathed out slowly.

He'd waited nearly ten years for this. Ten long years of working so hard that he would often fall asleep eating his evening meal. Unlike Margot, he'd had to start at the bottom. His jaw tightened. His job at Duvernay should have opened doors to him throughout the industry but, thanks to her family, that ladder had become a snake with a venomous bite.

After being more or less banished from France, it had taken him years to claw back his reputation. Years spent working punishingly long hours at vineyards in Hungary, and studying at night school until finally he had got a break and a job on an estate in California.

But every backbreaking second had been worth it for this, and although the shares had been expensive he would have paid double for this moment of reckoning.

His chest tightened. Finally he'd proved the Duvernays wrong!

He was their equal—for he was here, in their precious boardroom, not as some low-paid employee but as a shareholder.

He wanted to savour it. But although Margot looked suitably stunned—crushed, in fact, by his words—strangely, he was finding it not nearly as satisfying as he'd imagined he would.

Confused, and unprepared for this unexpected development, he stared at her in silence. And then immediately wished he hadn't, for with the light behind her, the delicate fabric of her white dress was almost transparent, and the silhouetted outline of her figure was clearly visible. It was almost as if she was naked.

A beat of desire pulsed through his veins.

Not that he needed a reminder. Margot's body was imprinted in his brain. He could picture her now, as he'd seen her so many times in those snatched afternoons spent in the tiny bedroom of his estate cottage. Lying in his arms, the curve of her belly and breasts gleaming in the shafts of fading sunlight, a pulse beating frantically at the base of her throat. Each time, he'd felt as though he was dreaming. He'd been completely in her thrall—overwhelmed not just by desire but by an emotion he had, until meeting her, always dismissed as at best illusory and at worst treacherous.

At first he'd tried to deny his feelings, had avoided her, and then, when avoiding her had become untenable, had been offhand almost to the point of being brusque, willing her to brand him rude and unapproachable if it meant hanging on to some small remnant of self-control.

But it had been so hard, for his body had been on fire, his brain in turmoil, all five senses on permanent high alert. He'd wanted her so badly, and for a time he'd believed that she wanted him in the same way. Insistently. Relentlessly.

Unconditionally.

And so he'd proposed—wanting, needing to make permanent that passion, that sense of belonging to someone, and of her belonging to him. He'd had no words for how he'd felt. It had defied description. All he had known was that he had a place in her life, her world. He had believed that unquestioningly. Only of course he'd been wrong.

Margot had wanted him, but her desire had been rooted in the transitory and finite nature of an affair—and more specifically in the illicit thrill of 'dating' her older brother's employee.

He felt anger spark inside him, and his eyes cut across the room to the line of portraits of Duvernays past and present.

Of course proposing to her had been his second mistake. His first had been to believe that his rapport with Yves was real, that it meant something. He had been lured not so much by the family's wealth and glamour, but by their sense of *contra mundum*, and the chance to be admitted into their world had been irresistibly potent to someone with his past.

With hindsight, though, he could see that his presence had always been subject to the grace and favour of the Duvernay family. They might have tolerated him, but he had never really belonged—just as Margot had never really belonged to *him*.

He felt his heart start to beat faster.

As a suitor, he'd always known that he was an underdog, a wild card—but, stupid and naive fool that he'd been, he'd actually respected her for seeing beyond his bank account and his background. Admired her for choosing him, for taking that risk. Now, though, he knew that the risk had been all his.

His hands trembled and he felt a rush of irritation at his naivety. No wonder he wasn't really *feeling* this moment. He might have created a business to rival theirs, but what had haunted him—and what still rankled and had made every relationship since Margot a short-lived and deliberately one-sided affair—was the fact that, just like his mother, he hadn't been good enough to marry.

The Duvernays might have welcomed him into their home, but ultimately they had never considered him worthy of permanently joining their inner circle. Not even Margot. *Especially not Margot.*

His head was suddenly pounding.

For nearly a decade he'd told himself that watching the House of Duvernay implode would be enough. Enough to erase the sting of humiliation and the pain of being so summarily cast out and ostracised. Only now, here, standing in this boardroom, it was clear to him that there was another, more satisfying revenge to be had: namely, seizing control of the business from Margot.

It was the only possible way to exorcise this lingering hold she had on him. To punish her as she deserved to be punished. For she had wronged him the most. Her betrayal was the most personal and the deepest.

His pulse twitched as for the first time he noticed the band on her wrist, his brain swiftly and efficiently deciphering the cursive writing. He felt warmth spread across his skin. And it just so happened that he knew the perfect way to make his revenge exquisitely and fittingly personal.

Exhilaration hit him like a shot of pure alcohol

and, resting his gaze on her profile, he steadied himself. 'I know how you must be feeling…'

Her head jerked towards him, her long pale blonde hair catching the light as it flicked sideways.

'I doubt that.' Dark brown eyes wide with anger and outrage locked on to his. 'Having feelings would make you human, and you clearly don't have an ounce of humanity.'

Staring at the pulse beating in the base of her throat, Max gritted his teeth. He had plenty of feelings for Margot, unfortunately most of them seemed to be occurring somewhere in the region of his groin.

Fighting off the frustration that was circling like a caged dog inside his head, Max took a step towards her. 'I *do* know. You might not have thought I had much to lose, but thanks to your brother I lost the little I had,' he said coolly.

Margot blinked. At the mention of her brother's name anger surged up inside her like a hot spring. 'Yves was protecting me.'

'Yes, by destroying me.'

She reeled back from the controlled fury in his voice. 'That wasn't his intention.'

'You think?'

She glared at him, not knowing what she hated more: the coolness in his eyes or the mockery distorting his beautiful mouth. 'Yes,

I do. He just did what any brother would do. I wouldn't expect you to understand that. I wouldn't expect you to understand feelings like loyalty and lo—

She broke off, appalled at what she had so nearly spoken out loud—not just the fact that she had loved him but loved him rapturously, with her body, heart and soul. Only her love had been unreciprocated—humiliatingly unilateral. Worse, it had blinded her to what he was really thinking.

A sudden sharp spasm of pain twisted her stomach, and the words he'd spoken to her so long ago suddenly echoed inside her head.

'It was all about the money. You and me. That's why I proposed. I just wanted your money.'

She felt his clear-eyed gaze probing her face, and more than anything she wanted to raise her hands and shield her eyes, conceal the emotions that were rising up inside her. But she wasn't about to give him the satisfaction of knowing how badly he'd hurt her. Or that the pain of his betrayal felt as fresh today as it had ten years ago.

Ignoring the thudding of her heart, she glared at him. 'Just because you don't care about anything but money—'

'You mean the money that you don't currently

have?' he said softly. 'Remind me, Margot. What is Duvernay's net to EBITDA ratio these days?'

Their eyes clashed, and she flinched inwardly at the anger and resentment taking shape in the no-man's land between them.

Forcing herself to stand her ground, she wrapped her fingers around her elbows. 'Why do you care? Or do you just want to gloat about that too?'

His face was still, but his eyes were glittering in a way that made the air thump out of her lungs. For a moment they stared at one another in silence, and then finally he shrugged. 'I wasn't gloating,' he said simply.

The mildness of his tone caught her off guard, for it was so at odds with the adversarial tension swirling around the room and inside her chest.

'I just like to be in full command of the facts. That's how I run my business.'

His eyes were fixed on hers, calm, appraising, unnerving, and she felt her breathing jerk, saw the muted colours of the walls slamming into focus.

'Well, luckily for me, whatever you might like to believe, Duvernay isn't your business,' she said, lifting her chin and returning his gaze, her brown eyes sparking with resentment.

How dare he do this? Saunter back into her life with his newly acquired shares and his careless gaze, unlocking the past and upending the present.

For a second there was total silence, and then his mouth curved slowly upwards. Despite herself, she felt her pulse flutter, for his smile was still so difficult to resist, and even though she wanted to deny its power she could feel a trembling heat starting to creep over her skin.

And he hadn't even touched her, she thought, her heart lurching against her ribcage.

'Well, *luckily for you*—' he paused, his eyes resting calmly on her face '—that could all be about to change.'

Abruptly his smile was forgotten, and she stared up at him in confusion, her skin tingling, mouth drying with fear and anticipation, trying and failing to make sense of his casual statement.

'All you need to do is say yes.'

His words hung in the air between them and she felt panic spread through her. Suddenly she was having to work hard to breathe. Her pulse gave a leap of warning. Something was happening—something undefined but important.

'Yes to what?' She was aiming for the same tone of neutral formality, but instead her voice sounded oddly hollow and strained.

Max held her gaze. He wanted to see her reaction. To watch the moment of impact. 'To marrying me.'

Margot gazed at him, rooted to the spot, her stomach clenching with shock. She knew her face had drained of colour, but she was too busy trying to quiet the chaos inside her head to care.

'Marry you!' Shaking her head, she gave a small, disbelieving laugh. 'You're crazy. Why would I want to marry *you*?'

'Is that a no?'

His face was closed, expressionless, but she could feel the anger rippling beneath his skin. Only she didn't care. Right now all she wanted to do was hurt him in the same way that he'd hurt her—was still hurting her. Or maybe not in the *same* way, for that would mean Max had a heart, and she knew from bitter, personal experience that wasn't the case.

But she could certainly puncture the beating core of Max Montigny—his masculine pride.

'A no? Of course not.' She glared at him, her own rage shocking her. 'Who could possibly resist a man like you, Max? I mean, it's every woman's dream to marry a lying, scheming hustler!'

Sarcasm did not come naturally to her any more than anger did, but coming so soon after her father's betrayal and the shock of seeing Max again his proposal was just too cruel, too painful.

Once, marrying Max had been her dream. When he and Yves had turned up for supper one evening she had looked up from her plate and just like that she had fallen in love. Actually, not fallen—it had been more like plummeting... like a star falling to earth.

His presence in her life had felt miraculous. The thrill of seeing him, talking to him, had been a new kind of bliss—both pleasure and pain—for he had been so smart and sexy, bewitchingly beautiful and impossibly laid back, and yet so unattainable. She had been desperate, hopeful, smitten—and then, unbelievably, it had happened.

Only she had never suspected why. Stupid, naive and crazily in love for the first time, she had never imagined the truth until that terrible afternoon when Yves had discovered them.

'Feeling better? Or do you want to start throwing punches as well as insults?'

Max's voice was as cold and toxic as nerve gas. Lifting her head, she cleared her throat, straightening her back, feeling the zip of her dress tingling against her spine.

'Sorry,' she said, without a hint of remorse. 'But I just can't imagine under what circumstances you think I'd ever, *ever*, even consider marrying *you*.'

His gaze didn't flicker. 'How about circumstances in which I agree to save your business?'

She stared at him, the sheer unexpectedness of his words making the edges of her vision watery. 'Save my business…?' she repeated slowly.

He nodded. 'If you agree to become my wife.' He paused, studying her face. 'It's up to you, of course.'

He was speaking with a mock courtesy that made her want to hurl her bag at his head.

'I can just leave. The choice is yours.'

Her skin was prickling and her heart was beating so loudly that it was getting in the way of her thoughts. 'That's not a choice,' she said hoarsely. 'That's blackmail.'

For what felt like a lifetime he stared at her thoughtfully, and then finally he gave a casual shrug.

'Yes, I suppose it is. But on some levels all business is blackmail.' His face was impassive, his eyes steady on hers. 'And that's what this is, Margot. It's just business.'

The truth, of course, was that he wanted to prove her and her family wrong. To demonstrate irrefutably that he *was* good enough to marry her. That his name was equal to hers. But his instincts warned him against revealing the truth, for surely it would show weakness to admit that their low opinion—*her* low opinion—still tormented him?

Besides, there was no need to reveal anything. Not when he already had a ready-made reason at his fingertips. Widening his stance, he focused his attention on the woman in front of him.

'Unlike yourself, I'm not in the habit of throwing good money after bad, and your father's shares are useless to me if Duvernay goes bankrupt.'

She took a breath, bracing herself as though for a blow. 'What has that got to do with marrying me?' she asked stiffly.

Tuning out the apprehension in her voice, he let her words echo around the room. 'Isn't it obvious? I'll marry you, and in return you'll give me your shares. That will make me the majority stakeholder in Duvernay and allow me to run the business as I see fit.' His mouth curled into a goading smile. 'By that I mean profitably.'

Her eyes narrowed. 'You're so arrogant.' Seething inwardly, Margot watched him gaze dismissively around the boardroom.

'It shouldn't be too hard. Frankly, I could turn this company around in a heartbeat.'

She gave a short, mirthless laugh. 'Wouldn't that require you to have a *heart*, though, Max?' she said sweetly.

He smiled. 'Oh, I have a heart, Margot—and

more importantly, unlike your brother, I also have a head for business.'

Her brown eyes narrowed. 'I don't want to know what you think about my brother any more than I want your money,' she spat.

He gazed down at her, unperturbed by her outburst. 'No, I'm sure you don't,' he conceded.

His eyes gleamed, the centres darkening so that suddenly it felt as though she was being dragged bodily into his pupils.

'But whether you want my money or not is largely irrelevant. The fact is, you need it.'

'I don't—' she began.

He waved her words away as though they were some kind of irritating insect. 'You do. And, frankly, the sooner the better. I'll give you free rein with the wedding arrangements…' he was watching her lazily, as though her consent was a foregone conclusion '…although I draw the line at wearing any kind of patterned waistcoat. So marry me, give me control over our destinies, and I'll make all your problems go away.'

'I doubt that. From where I'm standing, *you* are the biggest problem. You're conceited and selfish and utterly lacking in sensitivity.'

His smile widened. 'Presumably that's why I now own a quarter share of your business?'

Stifling an impulse to slap his smug, handsome face, Margot fixed her gaze on the gardens outside. How long was he going to carry on with this game? For surely that was all this talk of marriage was to him. A game designed to humiliate her further.

So stop playing it, then, she told herself irritably. *You're the CEO of a global business, not some dopey nineteen-year-old student.*

With a strength that surprised her, she turned and met his gaze head-on. 'I'm not going to give you my shares, Max,' she said flatly. 'And I'm definitely not going to marry you.'

His expression didn't change, but somehow she found that less reassuring rather than more, and moments later she realised why. She might have thought she was simply stating the obvious, but Max clearly thought she was calling his bluff.

'Is that right?'

She glared at him, her skin prickling with resentment—not just at his arrogance but at the beat of desire pulsing through her veins, and the knowledge that only Max had ever done this to her. Got under her skin and made her feel so off-balance. And the fact that he could still make her feel this way, that he still had this power over her, threatened her as much as his words.

She took a step back. 'Yes, it is,' she said quickly. 'You and I were a mistake I'm not planning on repeating. We're certainly not marriage material.'

'Why not? I'm a man…you're a woman. There are no obstacles preventing us from tying the knot.'

Jamming her hands into the pockets of her dress, she looked up at him, disbelief giving way to exasperation, then fury. 'Aside from mutual loathing, you mean?'

Glancing around the boardroom, he shook his head slowly. 'You see? This is why your business is struggling, baby. You're just too resistant to change, to new ideas.'

Her eyes narrowed. 'Oh, I'm sorry. I didn't realise blackmail was so on-trend!'

He laughed, and before she could stop herself— before she even knew she was doing it—she was laughing too. How could she not when his mouth curled up so temptingly at the corners, wiping the mockery from his face so that he looked heart-breakingly like his younger self?

And, fool that she was, she felt her pulse lose speed, felt a sudden overwhelming urge to reach out and touch the curve of his lips, to feel again the hard, masculine pressure of his body against hers.

Heat burned in her cheeks and she breathed in sharply. Her reaction had been instinctive, involuntary, but she was already regretting it.

How could she *laugh* with him after everything he'd done to her? And how could she let herself feel anything other than hatred and contempt for this man who was backing her into a corner, demanding something that was impossible for her to give?

She felt his gaze on the side of her face.

'What was that you were saying about mutual loathing?' he asked.

The mocking note was back, and she looked up defiantly, her whole body stiffening into fight mode. 'Just because you can make me laugh *once*, it doesn't mean anything.'

Dragging her gaze away from the indecently lush mouth, she stared past him.

Except that it did.

She winced inwardly. It was all there in her voice—everything that she didn't want him to hear or to know about how she was feeling—and that was why this conversation had to stop now.

'You might have a head for business, Max, but you have zero understanding of human nature. If—*if*—we were to get married, we wouldn't just be talking in the boardroom.' She felt a sudden prickle of ice run down her spine. 'We'd have to live together. Share a home.'

Share a bed, she thought silently, her face suddenly hot as his eyes narrowed on hers and something moved across the irises that made her breathing quicken.

Cheeks burning, she began speaking again. 'Share our lives. And how are we going to do that? We can't even be in the same room together without—'

But she never finished her sentence. Instead she made the mistake of looking up at him, and instantly the words stalled in her throat.

She felt her body tense, almost painfully, and then her legs started to shake just as they had the first time she had ever seen him. Dressed in faded jeans, a T-shirt that hugged the muscles of his arms, and wearing dark glasses, he had looked like a cocktail of one part glamour to two parts cool. And then he'd taken his glasses off, and it had been like a thunderclap bursting inside her head.

Over time she had, of course, grown used to how he looked. But at least once a day it had caught her off guard, and now apparently nothing had changed. The seemingly random arrangement of mouth, nose, cheekbones still had the same power to rob her of even basic impulses, such as breathing and speaking.

'Without what?'

Her stomach tightened with awareness. The air felt suddenly charged with a different kind of tension, and his voice had grown softer. Too soft.

She could feel it slipping over her skin like a caress, so warm and tempting and—

Deceptive! Had she really learned nothing from what happened between them?

Ignoring his eyes, she crossed her arms in front of her body, shielding herself from the pull of the past. 'It doesn't matter.'

'Oh, but it does. You see, I need an answer,' he said, and the smoothness of his voice in no way diluted his uncompromising statement.

'Well, tough!' Her eyes widened. 'You can't seriously expect me to give you one here and now?'

For a moment he didn't reply, just continued to stare at her thoughtfully, as though he was working out something inside his head.

'Actually, I can—and I am.'

Her pulse shifted up a gear as he glanced at the surprisingly understated watch on his wrist.

'Deals have deadlines, and this one runs out when I walk back out through that door.'

She took a breath, fear drumming through her chest. 'But that's not fair. I need time—'

'And *I* need an answer.'

The commanding note in his voice whipped at her senses so that suddenly her head was buzzing and the glare of the sunlight hurt her eyes.

'And, to be fair, you have had ten years.'

Margot blinked. 'You can't compare what happened then with this.' She felt suddenly sick. Surely he didn't think that this 'proposal' somehow picked up where they'd left off?

'This is nothing like before,' she said shakily.

'I agree. This is far better.'

She gaped at him speechlessly, uncertain of how to interpret his words, and then suddenly she shook her head, her eyes snapping upwards. 'Better! What are you talking about?'

Her voice was too loud. So loud that someone in the corridor would be able to hear her. But for the first time in her life she didn't care what other people might think.

'How is this better? How could this ever be better?'

'It's simpler. More transparent.' His gaze dropped to her throat, then lowered to the V of her dress. 'What you see is what you get. And, despite all your talk of mutual loathing, I think we can agree that we both like what we see.'

Margot felt something dislodge inside her. His closeness was making her unravel. She wanted to disagree. To throw his remark back in his face. Only she didn't trust herself to speak—not just to form the words inside her head but to say them out loud.

Her pulse hiccupped with panic, and his gaze cut to hers. Surely though he couldn't sense the way he made her feel?

But of course he could—he always had. And, as though reading her mind, he reached out and gently stroked her long blonde hair, his touch pulling her not just closer, but back to a past that she had never quite relinquished.

'I can't give you time, Margot, but I can give you a reason to marry me.'

His gaze rested on her face, his eyes drawing her in, and she felt her nerves quiver helplessly in response to the message in the darkening irises.

'You have given me a reason, Max,' she said shakily. 'It's called blackmail.'

There was a moment of silence, and then his gaze shifted from her eyes, dropping and pressing onto her mouth. Suddenly her skin felt too hot and too tight, and she had a slip-sliding sense of *déjà-vu* as he took another step closer, the intensity of his eyes tangling her breathing.

'Actually, I have a better reason.'

For perhaps a fraction of a second her brain was screaming at her to turn, to move, to run. And then his lips closed on hers and heat surged through her body as his arm curved around her waist. Her hands rose instinctively, palms pressing into the rigid muscles of his chest—but not to push him away. Instead her fingers curled into the front of his shirt and she was pulling him closer, even as his hand curled around her wrist.

The touch of his mouth, his hands, his body, was so familiar, so intoxicating, that she would have had to be inhuman not to respond. He was warm and solid and real—more real than anything else in the room, in the world.

It was impossible to deny, and he was impossible to resist...like drowning. The pain and the misery of the last ten years was fading into a pleasure that she had never expected to feel again, a pleasure she had only ever felt in Max's arms.

Something stirred in her head and she felt a kick of resistance.

Only it was all a lie, a cold-blooded seduction. He hadn't felt anything. Not then, and definitely not now.

And just like that the spell was broken. Heart still racing, she jerked her mouth free and pushed him away.

Resurfacing into the cool, sedate daylight of the boardroom, she felt heat burning her face. Only now it was the heat of humiliation. How had she let that happen? Why had she given herself to this man? A man who felt nothing for her and used her feelings as a weapon against herself.

Oh, he *wanted* her—but certainly not because he was powerless to do otherwise...

Skin burning, she took a step back and pressed

her hand against her mouth, trying to blot out the imprint of his lips, wishing there was a way she could erase him as quickly and permanently from her life and her memory.

But the truth was that even when she'd had every reason to do so she hadn't managed to wipe Max from her mind. And now she actually had a reason for him to be in her life.

Her pulse fluttered and she felt a momentary swirling panic rise up inside her chest like storm water. And then just as swiftly it drained away. This was not a time for feelings to get in the way of facts. And the facts were bleak.

The business was not just failing, it was heading for bankruptcy. And it wasn't just Duvernay the business that was facing ruin. If—no, *when* the business collapsed, her family would be thrown into the spotlight, humbled and humiliated. Worse, they would be homeless.

She didn't want to marry Max, but without his money her life and that of her family—the life they all took for granted—would not just be difficult, it would cease to exist. And how would she—how would *they*?—cope living like ordinary people?

Her heart contracted. They wouldn't. And she couldn't expect them to do so.

Briefly, she felt the weight of her responsibilities. For if this was to work then once again she would have to put her family before herself. To lie and keep secrets. But what choice did she have?

Right now, Max was her only option. Without him all would be lost.

Heat burned in her cheeks. But wasn't there just a tiny part of herself that was relieved to have Max there, going into battle alongside her? And, really, was marriage such a big sacrifice to make for the sake of your family and a two hundred year legacy?

She stilled her breathing, like a diver preparing to jump, and then, before she could change her mind, she said quickly, 'Okay, I'll marry you. But it has to look and feel real, like a traditional wedding. We'll need to talk about it properly.'

As an attempt to reassert her power it was pretty meaningless. She was in no position to demand anything—she knew it, and he knew it too—and yet she also knew instinctively that she couldn't allow herself to be a push-over.

She'd half expected him to rise to her challenge. Only he didn't. Instead he merely nodded, as though she'd asked him to email her an invoice rather than discuss the conditions of their marriage of convenience.

'Of course. I'll be in touch.'

And with that he turned, and suddenly she was alone.

She stared after him, her heart beating out of time, her limbs shaking with relief and a strange kind of excitement.

Finally he was gone—but of course she would see him again soon. Only that wasn't the reason why her heart was fluttering to the ground like a wounded bird. It was because the next time she saw him it would be as his fiancée.

CHAPTER THREE

Striding back into his Parisian hotel suite an hour later, Max tossed his phone carelessly onto one of the large velvet-covered sofas in the main living area.

He didn't know whether to feel elated or stunned.

Or just plain furious!

He should be on his way to Longchamp. He was due there to present a trophy to the winner of the big race, and normally he loved going to the races—whatever happened at the bookies, fast horses and beautiful woman were a winning combination.

But after leaving the Duvernay headquarters he'd got his PA to cancel. He'd had no choice. Margot had not only got under his skin, she was resonating inside his head. Her every word, every gesture, was running on a continuous loop like a live news feed from which it was impossible to turn away.

But why? He'd got what he wanted, hadn't he?

His mouth thinned. It should have all been so straightforward. A part of him had been planning some sort of revenge against the Duvernays for nearly a decade, painstakingly working towards the moment when finally he would prove to Margot, her brother, her whole damn family that they had been wrong about him.

And everything had been on schedule—right up until the moment she'd walked into the boardroom. His mind scrolled back to when he'd turned around and seen her in that dress—a dress that despite its couture credentials had somehow managed to conjure up memories of carefree summers, feel-good songs playing on car radios and the smell of hot bare skin.

Margot's hot bare skin.

He blinked. No wonder he'd been driven to act like that. Proposing marriage and then kissing her. His brain had been like bubble gum.

Frowning, he slid his hand under his tie and tugged it loose, before pulling it over his head and tossing it in the same direction as his phone. He felt tired, and the tension in his neck was making his back ache.

Infuriated by the devastating impact Margot had wrought on his mood and on his body, he slowly scanned the exquisite room, as though the opulent *fin de siècle* furnishings and huge gold-framed mirrors might offer up some kind of antidote. When that failed, he turned and stalked across the gleaming wood floor to the open French windows, stepping outside onto the roof terrace that adjoined his suite.

Directly opposite, the Eiffel Tower rose above the Paris skyline. Normally he found the sight of the city's most iconic monument inspirational for, like him, it too had initially struggled to be accepted before finally finding national and global fame.

Now, though, as he looked across at the familiar iron structure, it seemed oddly insubstantial.

His jaw tightened. A bit like the 'logic' that had driven his most recent actions.

He felt a rush of irritation, his shoulders tensing so that a spasm of pain nipped his spine. For 'logic' read 'libido'.

Barely registering the incredible three-hundred-and-sixty-degree views of the city, he gripped the balustrade, breathing out slowly as for maybe the hundredth time he ran through the morning's events, trying to disentangle the motives behind his behaviour.

Buying Emile's shares had been a luxury—overpriced and self-indulgent. Buying them, though, had served a purpose, for it had taken him to the Duvernay boardroom and a showdown with Margot.

A showdown that should have ended there.

And it would have ended there if he hadn't asked her to marry him.

Tilting his head back, he closed his eyes. At the time, marrying her and taking possession of her shares had seemed like a perfectly reasonable next step. The best and the only way to satisfy the hunger for revenge that had driven him back to France after nearly a decade.

Now, though, he could see that, whatever chain of events he had triggered in that boardroom, the truth was that his actions had been driven not just by a desire to possess Duvernay, but by a desire to possess Margot herself.

It had been if not a moment of madness then an act of impulse—an instinctive urge both to let go and move on from the past and at the same time continue that tantalising *pas-de-deux* with the only woman who had left an imprint on his soul. A woman who had burned him so badly that he had spent the intervening years running from the hurt, afraid to slow down and face his feelings, afraid to feel full-stop.

But for some reason, as he'd come face to face with her in that picture-lined room, he had decided not only to stop running but to re-stake his claim.

To what? he mocked. *Certainly not her heart.* She might have accused him of being cold-blooded, but Margot's heart lay buried beneath a layer of permafrost.

Opening his eyes, he gazed irritably across the skyline. None of this would have happened if he'd just stuck to the plan—only he'd had to go and let things get personal.

But of course he had. Because it was personal. Deeply and guttingly personal.

Margot had mattered to him like no other woman ever had. But then, she'd been like no other woman he'd ever known—and it hadn't just been about the sex. Before he'd met her he'd been so messed up—hungry for respect and respectability and yet resentful that he had to keep on earning it, asking for it, pushing for it.

She had been his serenity. His salvation.

His mouth thinned. Or so he'd believed until that evening when she'd tossed his proposal back in his face like a glass of wine. Ever since then he'd been carrying his pain and resentment like a dark storm cloud.

A storm cloud that had burst with a clap of thunder in that boardroom today.

But was it really that surprising? He might have bought the shares and engineered the meeting, but seeing her again had still been a shock.

Before she'd arrived he'd told himself she wasn't going to be as beautiful as he remembered, or as desirable. That kind of loveliness didn't last. But he'd been wrong—actually, more like deluded!

His body had responded to hers with a swiftness and an intensity that he'd never experienced around any woman except her. And as for her looks—

Well, he'd been wrong about that too.

Aged nineteen, she had possessed a beauty that had already been straining at the leash. With a pure clean-cut profile, pensive light brown eyes and almost ludicrously long legs, she'd been a mesmerising mix of coltish hesitation and a seriousness not common in one so young.

Today, though, she would not have looked out of place sashaying down the catwalk at Paris Fashion Week—or, better still, circling the paddock at Longchamp with all the other thoroughbreds. For she had outgrown or maybe grown into her long limbs, and there was no trace of that youthful hesitation. Only the soft half-pout and simply styled long, pale blonde hair still hinted at the girl he'd proposed to all those years ago.

He felt his pulse dart. Or it would have done if that girl had ever been real. But he knew now that she had only ever existed inside his head.

So who, then, was he marrying? And, perhaps more importantly, why was he prepared to go ahead with such an impulsive and ill-thought-out decision?

Breathing out slowly, his mind took him back to that first and last summer they'd spent together. A summer of love—secret, snatched love.

Margot had told him she needed to find the right moment to tell her family and, smitten with feelings that were powerful and compelling in their unfamiliarity, it had been an easy decision for him to go along with her wishes.

Cocooned together in the bedroom of the cottage that had come with his job, nothing had ever felt so good, so right—not even the first time he'd stepped foot in a vineyard.

It had been so new to him…so precious. He'd thought going public would end his bubble of happiness instantly. There would be no more just the two of them. Everything would change irrevocably.

His mouth curved downwards. Of course he hadn't anticipated quite how catastrophic that change would be—although maybe he'd always suspected the truth. That her secrecy and hesitation stemmed not from a desire to prolong the perfect private bliss of their affair, but from a belief that he was only good enough for sex, and that one day she would discard him like pomace—the unusable skins, pulp, seeds and stems from the wine grapes.

He was suddenly working to breathe.

This time, though, it would be different. This time there would be no sneaking around, no secrecy, no hiding him away.

If it had just been about recouping his money then, yes, he would have sat back and waited for her business to fail before stepping forward to scoop up the spoils. But why wait? Marrying her would have the same outcome, only it would be immediate—and it would be much more pleasurable.

Not only would he be in the driving seat at Duvernay, but Margot Duvernay—heiress and aristocrat of the wine world—would be his wife. His lawfully and very *publicly* wedded wife.

Gazing down at the city, he smiled happily, back no longer aching, suddenly immensely gratified with how the morning had played out.

Switching off the shower, Margot smoothed the water away from her face and silently breathed in the scented steam.

The camellia and jasmine body wash had promised to soothe her body and mind, but judging by the way her heart was still racing it clearly wasn't powerful enough to soothe away the aftershocks caused by the morning's events.

To be fair, though, she couldn't really blame the shower gel. Short of industrial quantities of alcohol. or maybe concussion, she wasn't sure that *anything* could counteract a close encounter with Max Montigny.

Chewing her lip, she wrapped a towel around her damp body, grateful for the comforting warmth and softness of its embrace.

Had anyone else bought her father's shares it would have been an awkward but bearable meeting, with a discussion followed perhaps by coffee. But instead it had been more like a gladiatorial battle, and there had been only one proposal on the agenda—Max's.

A proposal she had accepted.

Her pulse accelerated, and the saliva dried in her mouth as panic and fear at what she'd consented to do spiralled up inside her like a swarm of bees.

However, panicking wasn't going to change the facts—and they were simple. Not only had she agreed to transfer her shares to Max, she had also agreed to become his wife.

After he'd left she had briefly considered calling her lawyer. Only what would have been the point? She knew without even bothering to check that the contract he'd signed with Emile would be watertight.

Besides, right now, taking Max's money was the only way she could save her business *and* her family. And if that meant giving him her shares and marrying him, then that was what she would do.

She felt her stomach lurch, and some of her bravado began to ooze away. That was easy to say, but she couldn't pretend even to herself that the reality was going to be anything but challenging.

Glancing down at her wrist, she shivered. She could still feel his handprint on her skin, could remember the way their bodies had fitted together as they'd kissed, and the helpless, sightless oblivion of her passion.

Her hands fluttered involuntarily in her lap. Closing her eyes, she clutched the towel more tightly.

Her response to him wasn't that surprising, she thought defensively. And, given their history, surely she could forgive herself? The physical attraction between them had always been so overpowering and relentless that kiss had been inevitable. But, while her craving for Max might be understandable, even forgivable, giving in to it would only complicate things.

For the sake of her sanity and her pride it was clear that this deal would only work if she kept her feelings out of it. Viewed that way, she might just be able to believe that their marriage was simply another business transaction—a civilised, functional, mutually beneficial agreement between two consenting adults.

She felt her breath clog in her throat. All she needed to do now was believe her own sales pitch.

Opening her eyes, she stared slowly around her bedroom.

If only she had somebody she could confide in. It wasn't that she didn't have friends. She did. But friends were for fun—for nights out and playing tennis, going shopping. Telling them the truth about her life was just not an option. After so many years of keeping so much of the Duvernay drama under wraps, what would she say? Where would she start?

Nor could she share her fears and anxieties with her family, for they relied on her to be strong and steady and solicitous.

If only there was someone she could trust with her burden.

Her mouth twisted. *Like a husband.*

But, although her feelings for Max might be complicated and confusing, she knew with absolute certainty that she didn't trust him. Or at least that she only trusted him to hurt her.

Her pulse twitched and she felt a sudden urgency to move, to escape the loop of her thoughts. Stalking into the dressing room, she snatched a pair of faded blue jeans, a V-neck T-shirt and a pale grey ballet-style wrap.

If only she could just disappear. Get into her car and keep driving. Leave France, Europe—or better still become an astronaut…

She tugged the wrap around her waist and knotted it savagely. And do what?

She might escape Max, and the mess-in-waiting that was her business, but she would never escape her feelings. Even if she was floating hundreds of miles above the earth in a space station she would still be worrying about her family and trying to manage the chaos they produced.

That was what she did. What she'd always done since childhood, during the many evenings and weekends when her parents' volatile relationship had spilled over into a merry-go-round of accusations and denials.

When finally one of them—usually Colette—had stormed off in tears, it had been down to Margot to act as a go-between. And then, after they had inevitably retreated to the bedroom, it had been down to her to make up some story for the maids about how that vase had got broken, or why her father's clothes were scattered over the lawn. Yves, of course, was long gone, hiding out at a friend's house, and Louis had been a baby.

For a moment she stared silently at her reflection in the full-length mirror, seeing not herself but the dutiful little girl who had always done the right thing. Sorting out her parents' messes even if that had meant lying and keeping secrets.

And now she would be lying and keeping secrets for the rest of her life.

It would be easy simply to blame Max. *Marry me, or watch your business fail and your family end up homeless* was hardly much of a choice. But it wasn't that simple.

No one had made her go into the boardroom and face him. She could have got back into the lift, and sent in the lawyers. But some part of her had *wanted* to see him—and not just see him, she thought, her cheeks flaming as she remembered that kiss.

And Max hadn't come simply to gloat, or to pick out an office. He could have scheduled the meeting somewhere public, like a restaurant, but he had wanted to be alone with her too.

Looking down, she saw that her hands were shaking again. Theoretically, she knew that she should loathe him. But clearly her body hadn't received the memo about how it was supposed to behave when she met the man who had crushed her dreams and broken her heart.

It might make no sense, and even just thinking it made her feel helpless and angry, but although she might have to lie to everyone else she wasn't going to lie to herself. And the truth was that in spite of everything that had happened between them, and the fact that they no longer liked or trusted or respected one another, they still wanted each other with an intensity and desperation that overrode all logic and history.

Tipping her head back, she let out a long, slow breath. Perhaps, though, it was just the shock of seeing him again, she thought hopefully. Maybe when she saw him next time she would be immune to his charms.

She sighed. It didn't seem likely, but at least she wouldn't have long to find out.

The thought of seeing him again was making her heart pound so loudly that it took her some seconds to register that her phone was ringing.

She felt her muscles tense, her body pulling up sharply, like a horse refusing to jump a fence, and suddenly the air was humming around her.

Was it Max?

Instantly her heart gave a great leap, and as she walked swiftly back into her bedroom she gazed nervously down at the phone, oscillating from side to side on the polished surface of her dressing table.

But it was just Louis, calling from his week-long bachelor party in Marrakech.

Her heartbeat started to slow and she stared down at the screen, unnerved by the sharp sting of disappointment she felt at reading her brother's name. Usually she loved talking to her younger brother.

Louis had been too young to really register his parents' turbulent marriage so, unlike his older siblings, he had no memories of the past to colour his present. Instead he had inherited his parents' best qualities. Handsome and charming, like his father, he also had his mother's spontaneity. He was loved by everyone, and in return for this universal gift of love he wanted everyone around him to be happy. Particularly Margot.

The thought drove her back a step.

It was starting already. The lies and the secrecy. Only she wasn't ready. She wasn't ready to lie to Louis yet, she thought, panic blooming in her throat as her brain finally registered the tiny camera icon on the screen. And definitely not to his face.

But she was going to have to. For how could she suddenly just announce that she was going to marry a man she had never so much as mentioned before?

Louis would be stunned, devastated and hurt. Just picturing the lines of his face made her heart contract painfully and she felt a flicker of despair. Would it never end? Would she ever be free to just live?

Her pulse accelerated.

She could almost picture Max's handsome

face. Could hear his soft, goading voice daring her to make a choice.

Her hand hovered over the phone and then, cursing softly, she took a quick, sharp breath and picked it up, swiping her fingers across the screen.

'Louis! How lovely to hear from you!'

Her breath ached in her chest as she smiled down at her brother's face.

'How's Marrakech?'

'It's amazing. I feel like I'm on a movie set.'

She smiled. His face was so unguarded, so flushed with happiness, and she felt some of the tension inside of her loosen.

'Well, I got the photos you sent and it looks beautiful,' she said truthfully. 'Are you having fun?'

'Of course. You know, I can't believe you haven't been out here.'

Louis sounded genuinely confused, and Margot experienced the sensation that she often did when speaking to her brother—a kind of shock that she was related to such a normal, well-balanced person. To him, Marrakech was just a beautiful, glamorous destination. The perfect backdrop for a week of hedonism. The fact that his family owned a former palace in the old city was just a bonus and a happy coincidence.

To her, though, the Palais du Bergé would always be the place where her parents had fled after their many rows—only Louis didn't need to know that.

And that was the other reason she'd agreed to marry Max. Louis needed protecting from the truth, and Max's money and her silence would make sure that continued to happen.

When the time was right she would give him an expurgated version of the last few days. But right now she was just grateful for the chance to think about something other than Max's life-changing reappearance in her life.

She cleared her throat. 'Oh, you know—I've just never really got round to it. Too busy at work. But let's not talk about that now. Tell me what you've been up to.'

'I'm not ringing to talk about me, Margot.'

Louis looked and sounded so uncharacteristically stern that she found herself smiling. 'So who *do* you want to talk about?'

'I want to talk about you, and why you're in France when you're supposed to be in Monaco. Is this your way of telling me that you still don't approve of me getting married?'

Margot grimaced, guilt digging her beneath the ribs. With all the drama with Max, she had completely forgotten about Gisele and Monte Carlo.

'No, of course not,' she said quickly. 'And I

never didn't approve. I was just worried—you're both so young.'

She had been worried at first, but although both Gisele and Louis were impulsive and indulged, they lacked the self-absorption and wilfulness of her parents—and, more importantly, their relationship was not simply based on sex.

'So why did you leave?'

The petulance in her brother's voice was fading, but he was still frowning.

'Oh, Louis, I'm sorry. I really did want to stay, only something came up—'

'Something or *someone*?'

She froze, his words slamming into one another inside her head. Her body reacted instinctively, like a hare spooked by the shadow of a hawk, stilling and shrinking inwards as her legs gave way beneath her and she slid noiselessly onto the bed.

Damn Max! Had he spoken to Louis? Had he spoken to her grandfather as well? And, if so, what had he said to them?

'So? Are you going to tell me what he wanted or not?'

Louis's voice was impatient now, but she hardly registered the shift, so great was her misery at the way all the parts of her life that she'd worked so hard to keep separate were now suddenly and violently converging.

'Yes, of course.' The smile on her face was starting to hurt, and it was an effort to force herself to speak. 'I just didn't want to bother you while you were away. I thought it would just be easier if I handled it—him—on my own.'

She heard her brother sigh. 'He knows how to pick his moments, doesn't he? I mean, he makes no effort to have any sort of relationship with me, and then when I'm not even in the country he just randomly leaves me a message.'

Margot blinked in confusion. 'What message?'

Louis frowned. 'Exactly! *What* message? It was just him drinking and talking rubbish. Except for the part when he said that he didn't really want to talk to me. That he was just trying to get hold of you and he couldn't.' There was a moment's silence. 'So what was it then? What was so incredibly urgent that the great Emile Lehmann actually deigned to call *me*?'

For a moment she couldn't speak. Her whole body felt weak, buffeted by a fast, wild, rushing relief, and she badly wanted to laugh. Only suddenly it felt horribly close to wanting to cry—for what if she'd actually blurted everything out?

Tightening her grip around the phone, she took a breath and said as casually as she could manage, 'He just wanted to talk about a business venture.'

'You mean he wanted money? Seriously, Margot. Did he know where you were, or what you were doing there?' He shook his head, exasperation in his voice. 'No, of course not. I mean, why would he know anything about my life? I'm only his son.'

She bit her lip, for now there was more than exasperation, there was pain too.

After she and her brothers had gone to live with her grandparents, Yves had refused to see Emile any more. He had always distanced himself from their parents' behaviour, so maybe he'd thought distancing himself from a father he considered weak and embarrassing was the next logical step.

Her grandparents had seemed to think so too, and had done nothing to dissuade him. Nor had they encouraged Louis to stay in contact with his father. In fact it had been Margot alone who had kept in touch with Emile.

She breathed out softly. She knew her father should have done more. But her grandparents had made it so difficult for him that inevitably he'd given up. It was all so stupid and senseless—but that didn't mean that Louis wasn't hurt by the fact that their father only ever talked to her.

'It wasn't just business,' she said quickly. 'He wanted to get you and Gisele a wedding present.'

The lie was so swift and slick that for a moment she almost believed it herself. And, of course, by the time the wedding happened she would have chosen a gift, coaxed Emile into sending it, and then it wouldn't be a lie any more.

'I think he felt awkward.'

She felt suddenly tired. How had she become this person? Not only was she able to lie to her own brother without flinching, she already knew the arguments she would use against herself later to rationalise her behaviour.

'He said that?' Louis looked at her uncertainly, but he sounded somewhat appeased. 'I'm surprised he even remembered I'm getting married.' He paused. 'But why did that mean you had to leave Monte Carlo?'

She didn't blink. Instead she stared across her bedroom at the Renoir lithograph of a young woman that had been a gift from her grandfather for her twenty-first birthday. It had always been one or her favourite pictures, and now she found the girl's calm expression particularly comforting.

'There was a problem at work,' she said quickly. 'Me coming back had nothing to do with Emile. It was just a coincidence.' She hesitated. 'Did Gisele mind?'

'A little. But she didn't actually think you would go at all, so—'

'I wanted to go,' she protested. 'And I would have stayed. I was having fun.'

'Liar!' Louis burst out laughing. 'You hate themed parties.'

She started to laugh too, and for a moment it was just the two of them, and life was simple and sunny again. 'True, but I'm only human—and there's something strangely irresistible about a lace body stocking and fingerless gloves.'

She'd wanted to hear her brother laugh again, and listening to his whoop of delight she felt a rush of pure, uncomplicated love for him.

'Please tell me there are photos.'

She smiled. 'Maybe! But what happens on bachelorette week stays on bachelorette week.'

'So, did you sort it out?'

The shift in topic caught her off guard, and it took a moment for her to understand the question. Without even meaning to do so Louis had introduced Max into the conversation, and just like that she was back in the boardroom, her body just inches from his, the pull between them like a living, pulsing force of nature...

Quickly pushing the image aside, she cleared her throat. 'Yes—it's all sorted.'

Her heart began to pound. *Was it?* Did agreeing to marry a man you loathed simply to save your family from public humiliation count as sorted?

Yes, she thought fiercely. It did. It might not be the future she'd pictured, but it would be far better than any she could produce without Max's investment.

'My sister the big-shot boss.'

Louis sounded gleeful. He had no interest in the business, but his admiration of Margot was partisan and unquestioning, and she felt another rush of love for him.

'You are *so* going to give this new *terroiriste* a run for his money. Have you met him yet?'

Margot frowned. The term wasn't new to her. There was a growing movement among wine-growers around the world that wines should be a unique expression of soil and climate—not a result of artificial intervention from chemical pesticides and fertilisers. She had been try-ing for years to push Duvernay to become more biodynamic, but change had been slower than she would have liked, because change required money that she simply didn't have.

Her pulse twitched, and she realised that her thought process was inching dangerously back towards Max and that conversation in the boardroom. With another effort of will she dragged her mind back to Louis's impatient, handsome face.

'Have I met who? What are you talking about?'

'You know—this Max Montigny. Guillaume had a chat with him at the country club and he told him that he's looking to move into the region. Apparently he's already got his eye on one of the big champagne estates.'

For a moment Margot couldn't speak. The shock of hearing Louis say Max's name out loud was just so deep and sudden. Only not as much of a shock as learning that Max's intentions were a matter for public discussion. Somehow that made everything feel a little sharper, more in focus. More urgent.

She pressed a fingertip against the side of her head, pushing down on the pain that had begun pulsing there. 'What did Guillaume think?'

Guillaume was Gisele's father, a genial industrialist who had made a fortune in telecommunications and was now looking to move into politics.

'What? About Montigny? Oh, he liked him—but he said he couldn't figure him out. That he looked like a film star but sounded like a banker. Until he started talking about wine. And then he sounded like a revolutionary.' Louis paused, as though he couldn't figure Max out either. 'But I don't think you need to worry about him, Comtesse du Duvernay.'

She smiled automatically. It was a childhood

nickname. Yves and Louis had used to call her that whenever they'd thought she was being too bossy. Only now it felt like a cruel joke—an empty title for a woman who had traded herself like a chattel, marrying not for love but money.

'Is that right?' she said quickly, forcing a lightness into her voice that she didn't feel.

Louis grinned, the tiny screen barely diminishing the infectious power of his smile. 'Damn right, it is. If anyone can handle him it'll be you.'

After she'd hung up Margot blow dried her hair, and applied her make-up with careful precision. Glancing in the mirror, she felt her stomach clench. She might be CEO of one of the biggest champagne producers in the world, but this was her real skill. Presenting an image of serenity and control to the world while inside chaos reigned.

With an effort, she tried to arrange her thoughts to match her outward composure, but Louis's words kept stubbornly weaving through her head like the subtitles to a movie she didn't want to watch.

Film star. Banker. Revolutionary.

Blackmailer.

She gritted her teeth. It sounded like a warped child's nursery rhyme, but in fact it was just another reminder of how little she knew Max. And,

despite her brother's faith in her, of how ill-pre-
pared she was to manage him.

Her throat tightened. But then she wasn't just
managing Max, was she? She was marrying
him.

CHAPTER FOUR

'WOULD YOU LIKE sparkling or still water?'

Glancing up from the bread roll she had spent far too long buttering, Margot smiled politely at the waiter. 'Still, please.'

She glanced across the table to where Max was discussing the wine with the hotel's sommelier. They were having lunch in his hotel suite. He had texted her an hour earlier, telling her what time to arrive, and although she was irritated by the no doubt deliberate short notice she was grateful not to have to prolong the agony, and relieved that he'd suggested lunch and not dinner.

Although now she was here she couldn't help feeling on edge, for being summoned to his rooms had made her feel like some kind of concubine.

Carefully, she laid her knife across her side plate. He had also—and this time she had no doubt that he'd done it deliberately—omitted to tell her where he was staying.

Of course he hadn't been hard to find. Judging by the amount of column inches given over to his presence in Paris, Max Montigny's whereabouts were not just a key piece of information to her, but a matter of fascination to most of the French public.

Her heartbeat twitched.

His casual, arrogant assumption that she'd have no choice but to track him down made her want to reach over and slap his beautiful face. But what did it matter, really? In the wider scheme of things it was just another hoop for her to jump through—a nudge to remind her that he was in charge. Not that she really needed the balance of power in their relationship to be pointed out. Every humbling second of yesterday's meeting was seared onto her brain.

But, although it been painful and humiliating to have to accept his proposal, of the many emotions she was feeling the one that was overriding all others was not anger, nor even misery, but oddly relief. Since Max had offered to marry her and turn her business around, for the first time in the longest time some of the crushing burden of responsibility she'd been carrying around seemed to have lifted from her shoulders.

Finally there would be somebody by her side. Somebody who would have her back. She shivered. If still felt strange, though, putting her life and her family's future into the hands of Max Montigny.

Her mouth felt suddenly dry.

If only the secrecy and lies surrounding their arrangement had felt equally unfamiliar. But they hadn't. Instead everything—the half-truths she had told her grandfather about where she was going, her decision to drive herself and thus not include her chauffeur in the deception—had all conspired to make time contort.

And the unsettling sensation of past and present blurring hadn't gone away when, having kept her waiting for ten minutes, Max had finally strolled into the room, dressed casually in jeans and a grey T-shirt.

His lateness had been as deliberate as his failure to tell her where they were meeting, and she had found it just as provoking, but that wasn't the reason her heart had begun beating faster.

Watching him move towards her, with a languid purpose that had made her stomach tighten painfully, she had been forced to face the truth. That her body's response to him in the boardroom had been no one-off. And that, even while she loathed him, his beauty could still reduce the world around her to mere scenery.

'Good.'

Max's voice cut into her confused thoughts and, looking up, she felt her eyes bump into his.

Instantly, she felt a rush of nerves, as though she was about to tackle the Cresta Run instead of merely eat lunch.

'Thanks, Jean-Luc.' His gaze never leaving her face, he dismissed the sommelier with a nod of his dark head. 'I hope you don't mind but I thought it would be easier if I selected the wine.' The corners of his mouth twitched. 'Save any arguments.'

'Of course,' she said tightly, her heart banging against her chest. 'What did you choose?'

'A Clement-Dury Montrachet to start, and then a Domaine-Corton Pinot Noir to follow.'

'I like them both,' she said truthfully. 'Especially the Montrachet. It has such a good finish.'

Max grinned suddenly, and the unguarded excitement in his eyes caught her off-balance.

'It does, doesn't it? I like the balance of flavours—and that citrus really resonates.' He picked up the wine menu and flicked through it idly. 'They've got a great list here...really strong on small producers.' His face grew mocking. 'Although, rather embarrassingly for them, the management turned me down when I was starting out.'

Margot looked at him blankly, caught off guard by his remark, for—just like the rest of his life—Max's dizzyingly rapid rise to success was a mystery to her.

'It must have been hard for you,' she said cautiously. 'It's amazing…what you've done.'

He shrugged. 'I worked hard, and it helped that we got some outstanding reviews in the wine press.'

She nodded, but she hardly took in his words. She was too distracted by the speed with which their relationship was moving. Yesterday they had been hurling the verbal equivalent of thunderbolts at one another, and yet here there were today, talking almost normally, just like any other couple having lunch.

Tearing off a piece of her roll, she slid it into her mouth and forced herself to chew. And that was what she'd wanted, wasn't it? A civilised arrangement, free from unsettling feelings and even more unsettling actions.

Her skin grew warm as once again she remembered that kiss in the boardroom, remembered pleasures buried but not forgotten, the glowing imprint of his lips and fingers on her skin…

The sommelier returned at that moment and, heart pounding, she waited for him to pour the wine into their glasses. When finally they were alone again she said crisply, 'Is that why you chose this place?' She made herself look across at him. 'Or was it the allure of the black door?'

She was referring to the famous hidden entrance to the building, which allowed the ho-

tel's A-list clientele and their overnight guests
to come and go without having to face the in-
truding lenses of the paparazzi.

His mouth curled upwards. 'The former, I'm
afraid. Sadly, I don't have anything or anyone
to hide from the press.' He made a show of hesi-
tating, his eyes glittering with amusement. 'Oh,
I'm sorry. Was that the Duvernay way of telling
me that you're planning on staying over?'

She glared at him, torn between fury at his
arrogance and despair at the lurch of heat his
words produced.

Picking up another piece of bread, she mashed
butter into it savagely. 'If you seriously believe
that, then you must have an awfully vivid imagination.'

He stared at her across the table. His expression was still pleasant and interested, but there
was a definite tension in the air.

'I don't need an imagination to remember
what it's like between us, Margot.'

Her body felt suddenly soft and boneless. She
knew he was talking about what had happened
in the boardroom, but she deliberately chose to
misinterpret him.

'I'll have to take your word on that,' she said
stiffly. 'What happened between us was such a
long time ago and so brief I can barely remember it.'

'Really?'

The word slid over her skin like a caress, and he gave her a smile that made the edges of her vision start to blur. Breathing in unsteadily, she curled her fingers into her palms, feeling her skin tighten with shame at how easily she had succumbed to the pull of the past. At how even here, now, her body was responding to his with a hunger and a lack of judgement that was both undeniable and humiliating.

As though reading her thoughts, he leaned forward, his eyes resting on her face, watching the colour spread slowly over her cheeks.

'Then your memory must be *awfully* poor, indeed. Or just in need of refreshing, perhaps.'

For a second they both stared at one another, and then he picked up his wine glass. '*À ta santé.*'

The meal was perfect. The hotel's chef was renowned, and clearly he was determined to impress. Ratte potatoes topped with a mousseline of smoked haddock and Sologne caviar was followed by turbot with wild pink garlic in a brown butter zabaglione. There was an array of seasonal regional French cheeses, and to finish an iced coffee parfait with a lemongrass-infused chocolate sorbet.

Laying down her cutlery, Margot felt sudden panic squeeze her chest. Throughout lunch the constant presence of the staff had prevented any long, awkward silences, and she had been able to smile and chat quite naturally. But now the meal was coming to an end, and as the waiters quietly left the room, she felt her pulse start to accelerate.

Being alone with Max had been difficult enough when she'd been shocked and angry. Now, though, the shock had faded, and her anger was at best intermittent—like Morse Code.

Unfortunately, what hadn't faded was her susceptibility to his beauty and sexuality. Her shoulders stiffened. But even if she couldn't control her body's response to him, she certainly didn't have to act on it.

Yes, she might have agreed to become his wife, but there was a huge difference between what was legal and what was *real*. Their wedding might be legal, but it would be purely for show. No ceremony, lawful or otherwise, could stop Max being the man who was blackmailing her into marriage—in other words, her enemy.

Remembering again that near-miss kiss in the boardroom, she shivered. Except what kind of enemies kissed?

Picking up her glass, she took a sip of wine. She wasn't going to think about that now. All she wanted to do at this moment was get through this meal, discuss the terms of their agreement and then leave.

Her mouth twisted. That, at least, was different from the past.

Back then she and Max had been desperate to be alone. To have privacy to talk, to touch, to laugh, to listen. But there had always been people around them—estate workers, guests staying at the chateau, and of course her family. Back then it had been like a kind of torture to have to remember that they were 'just friends', and that she couldn't touch him as she did in private.

Quashing the memory of just how much she had liked to touch him in private, she looked up and found Max watching her appraisingly, the blue and green of his gaze so level and steady that her heart began banging inside her throat.

Hoping that her face revealed nothing of her thoughts, and eager to be away from his scrutiny, she said stiffly, 'Shall we take coffee in the lounge?'

To her relief, he nodded, but as she walked into the large, opulent sitting room she swore silently. It was bad enough there were no armchairs, but the curtains had been drawn against the piercing afternoon sun, and there was something about the shadowy room and the sleek black velvet sofas that made her stomach flip over—some hint of a private salon, of soft breathing and damp skin...

Summoning up what she hoped was a casual

smile, she sat down. Seconds later she felt him drop down beside her, as she'd known he would, and then his weight tipped her slightly sideways, and she felt her pulse stumble as his leg brushed against hers.

Instantly the hairs on her arms stood up, and it took every ounce of willpower she had not to lean into the heat and hardness of his thigh and press her body against his.

Shaken by the close contact, shocked by the explicitness of her thoughts, she turned and stared quickly across the room to the gap between the curtains.

Outside the window Paris was all pink blossom and golden sunlight. It was the most perfectly romantic of backdrops and her heart began to beat faster, for it seemed so glaringly at odds with what she and Max were agreeing to do.

'Coffee?'

She blinked, then nodded, but in truth her mind was already slipping away—back to the memory of another sunlit afternoon and another cup of coffee.

It had been a moment of rare impulsiveness. Knowing it was Max's day off, she had gone to his cottage alone. She had felt bold and reckless—in short, nothing like her normal self. But when Max had finally opened the door, shirtless, his eyes neither green nor blue but somewhere in between, her bravado had fled, her body stilling, her mind blank with panic. Because that was as far as she'd got inside her head.

Everything else had been just a fantasy.

And maybe it would have stayed a fantasy—only, incredibly, Max had asked her in and made her a cup of coffee. A cup of coffee that had sat and gone cold while her fantasy became real. Or so she'd thought at the time.

She cleared her throat. 'Just black. Thank you.'

'When did you drop the sugar?'

Drop the sugar? She stared at him blankly. Was that some kind of code or slang?

He raised an eyebrow. 'You used to take sugar.'

It was not quite a question, and his voice sounded softer, almost teasing, as though the nod to their shared past had softened his mood.

But it wasn't fair of Max to change the tone from *sotto* to *scherzando* without warning. Nor was it fair of him to smile like that, she thought helplessly, her eyes drawn inexorably to the slight fullness of his lower lip. It wasn't fair of him to remind her of the past she'd worked so hard to forget. A past that hadn't even been real.

She cleared her throat.

'Yes, I did.' She nodded. 'But I stopped putting it in my coffee a few years ago. In fact, we barely eat any sugar at home any more—extra sugar, I mean.'

Max stared at her in silence, his face showing none of the emotion that was tearing through his chest.

Watching her talk, he had forgotten just for the briefest of moments why she was there. Forgotten why 'it'—the two of them—had ended all those years ago. Instead, he could only think of the reasons it had started.

Her smile. Her laughter. Her brain. He'd loved that she was smart—not just book-smart, although she had always been that but perceptive in a way that had suggested she was far older than nineteen.

And her body.

Useless to lie. He was a man, and what normal heterosexual man wouldn't respond to that arrangement of contours and curves and clefts. His heart thumped against the roof of his mouth and an answering pulse of desire started to beat in his groin.

Ignoring the heat breaking out on his skin, he forced himself to speak. 'Any particular reason?'

Margot shrugged. She hadn't expected him to pursue the topic, and suddenly she was grappling with how much to give away. Her grandfather's poor health was not common knowledge, but to give no answer would be just as revealing.

'My grandfather had a stroke about six months ago,' she said flatly. 'Modifying his diet was something the doctors suggested we do afterwards.' She took a deep breath. 'But I'm sure you didn't invite me here to talk about my grandfather's diet.'

Glancing down at her diamond-set wristwatch, she lifted her chin.

'And I know you must be as busy as I am. So perhaps we should start discussing the terms of our arrangement?'

Max felt himself tense. If he'd needed a reminder as to why their relationship had always been a non-starter it was there in those sentences, he thought on a rush of fury and resentment. For even now, when she was here *only* at his bidding, she still couldn't stop herself drawing a line in the sand, pointedly shutting him out of anything that trespassed on Duvernay matters and bringing the conversation back to business.

Briefly he considered telling her that the deal was off. That if she wanted money that badly there was a bank two doors down from the hotel and another one on the next street. But then he felt his pulse slow.

Looked at differently, Margot had done him a favour, reminding him of what mattered to her: her business and her bloodline. Both of which had been off-limits to a nobody like Max—until now.

He let his gaze drift slowly over her face. 'From memory, it was less of an invitation and more or an instruction,' he said softly. 'Or do you still think you have some say in what's happening here?'

Her eyes flared and he felt a beat of satisfaction, watching her struggle to stay calm.

'Fine! You told me to come,' she retorted, a note of frustration sharpening her voice, 'and I'm here. So, are we going to discuss our marriage or not?'

He lounged back, the shadow of stubble on his jawline co-ordinating perfectly with the velvet nap of the sofa. 'We are,' he said finally, his eyes never leaving her face, 'but first I want to give you this.'

Reaching into his jacket, he pulled out a small, square box.

His mouth curled into a mocking smile. 'Don't get too excited. It's from necessity, not any sort of romantic impulse on my part. You'll need to wear it. In public, at least.'

Flipping open the lid, he dropped the box carelessly into her open hand.

There was a short, spiralling silence.

Gazing down, Margot felt her stomach clamp tight, like a vacuum sealing inside her. The ring was beautiful. A huge yellow diamond flanked by two smaller white diamonds. And yet for some reason she couldn't seem to take it in. Instead she could feel herself being dragged back in time, to the moment when Max had stood in front of her, a pear-cut sapphire set in a band of gold in his outstretched hand.

It had been the most exciting moment in her life.

And the most terrible.

The picture was frozen inside her head. Max, his face expressionless, herself, silent and rigid with shock. And then Yves strolling in, his easy smile twisting, his mood turning from sweet to sour in the blink of an eye, shouting accusations and threats, teeth bared like a cornered dog.

Her brother's anger had been shocking, awful, brutal. But not as brutal as Max's admission that none of it had been real. That he'd only ever wanted her for her money.

'It's beautiful.' She knew her voice sounded stilted, fake, but it was all she could manage.

Max studied her face. It was his own fault. For years he'd wanted to believe that he'd been wrong. That she had really wanted to be his wife, and that given the opportunity—

He gritted his teeth. But of course he'd been right the first time. Yves's intervention had merely brought things to a head. Showing not a flicker of emotion, he said quietly, 'I'm glad you like it.'

Margot looked up. Something in his voice elbowed aside the promise she'd made not to ask about his personal life. She couldn't help the sudden swirling riptide of curiosity from rising up inside her, for of course she was curious.

And so, in spite of her intention to stay silent, she found herself saying, 'It's lucky neither of us had other commitments.'

She held her breath, waiting for an answer, a sharp needle of jealousy stabbing beneath her heart.

Max felt something heavy dragging down inside of him. If only he could reach across and shake that fixed, polite smile from her mouth. Or maybe it was himself he wanted to shake—anything to shift the dark, leaden ache in his chest.

Watching her, he felt his breath tangle into knots. Luck had nothing to do with it. After Margot he'd had relationships—no-strings, sexually satisfying affairs that had helped ease the sting of her rejection. But work had been his real commitment, for there he had been able to harness his anger and resentment, and that had driven the ambition that had taken him back to France and to that meeting with Emile.

Clearing his throat, he bit down on the anger rising inside him. 'Don't you mean lucrative?' he said coolly.

Her head jerked up, and the stunned, helpless expression on her face made something claw at him inside. But he told himself he didn't care, and pretending he'd noticed nothing, he smiled casually.

'I've picked out wedding rings for both of us, so all you need to do is speak to your family,' he continued relentlessly. 'Tell them that you'll be away for a couple of days. Oh, and you'll need a dress.'

'Away where? And why do I need a dress?' She frowned suspiciously.

He raised an eyebrow. 'To get married in, of course. We leave for the Seychelles tomorrow.'

She gazed at him in wordless disbelief, a flutter of fear skittering down her spine. 'Tomorrow?'

His eyes were cool and mocking. 'What?' he asked softly, and she could hear the taunting note in his voice. 'Did you think I was going to wait another ten years?'

Her head was suddenly aching and her vison was going watery at the edges. She opened her mouth, then closed it again. Her brain seemed to have stopped functioning. 'This is a joke, right? I mean, you can't expect me to marry you *tomorrow.*'

'I don't. The paperwork won't be ready in time.' The upward curve of his mouth was like a fish hook through her heart. 'I do, however, expect you to marry me in three days.'

For a moment she could only stare at him in stunned silence. And then finally she shook her head, her blonde hair flicking from side to side like a lioness's tail. 'I don't care about what you expect,' she snapped, her eyes clashing with his. 'That isn't going to happen.'

Over the last twenty-four hours she had, if not fully adjusted to her fate, at least accepted the benefits of marrying Max. But as far as she was concerned telling her family was a long way off. She'd anticipated an engagement period of several months, during which time she would have got her grandfather and Louis used to the idea of Max as her boyfriend, then her fiancé. Now, though, the option of gently breaking her future plans to them was not just under threat, it was in pieces.

She shivered. Her stomach felt as though it was filling with ice.

For most people a wedding in an exotic location with few legalities and a minimal waiting time would probably sound spontaneous and romantic. To her, though, it sounded like an exact duplicate of her parents' hasty elopement.

But she couldn't explain that to Max. Not without revealing more about herself than she was willing to share with a man who was not only blackmailing her into marriage, but was incapable of even the most basic human empathy.

She gazed at him stonily. 'Surely you can understand that? I mean, what exactly am I supposed to tell my family? I can't just roll up and announce that I'm getting married.'

He shrugged. 'Come, come, Margot. You're a Duvernay. You can do what you like. Besides, you've had a lot of practice in lying. I imagine you'll think of something.'

The rush of fury was intoxicating. Suddenly she was on her toes like a boxer, fingers twitching, clenching and unclenching. 'You unspeakable pig—'

He cut across her, his voice razor-edged and cold as steel. 'Spare me the outrage. You lied to your family for months about our relationship last time. Now you only have to do it for three days.'

'Wasn't it lucky that I did?' she snarled. 'At least they were spared *your* lies and deceit.'

There was a charged silence. He didn't reply, just continued to sit there, his face taut, his eyes impassive. And then, just as she was about to demand a response, he abruptly stood up and with careless, unhurried ease, walked to the door and yanked it open. Stepping aside, he stared coolly back across the room, his jawline and cheekbones suddenly in shadow.

'Let me make this simple for you, Margot. Either you agree to marry me in three days or you walk through this door now and take your chances with the bank.'

His tone was pleasant, but there was no mistaking the ultimatum in his voice.

Margot gazed at him in silence, her heart skidding sideways like car on black ice. Surely he was calling her bluff. He had to be. And yet she couldn't bring herself to find out, for if she got up and walked towards the door it was just possible that she would lose everything.

She had no weapons to bring to the fight, and escalating things would only make that fact obvious to Max. All she could do was back down with as much dignity as she could manage.

'Since you put it so charmingly,' she said stiffly, ignoring the heartbeat that was telegraphing frantically inside her chest, 'I'll do it.' She lifted her chin, her brown eyes locking on to his face, staring him down. 'But on one condition.'

'Condition?'

She heard the hint of surprise in his voice, and felt a fleeting quiver of satisfaction. 'Yes, damn you.' Matching his level, assessing gaze with what she hoped was one of her own, she gave a humourless laugh. 'What did you think? That I'd just bow down to your threats and intimidation?'

Max let his eyes drift over her face, seeing both the pulse quivering at the base of her throat—that beautiful, graceful throat—and the discs of colour spreading over her cheeks. No, he hadn't thought that, and in a way he hadn't wanted it either. He would never want that from this woman who had been like a living flame in his arms.

Casually he pushed the door shut and walked across the room, stopping in front of her. 'Name it,' he demanded.

'As soon as we're married I want to tell my grandfather and brother in person—before details are released to the press.'

The marriage would be a shock to both of them, but she knew that they would accept and understand it better if she told them herself.

Max stared down at her, trying to ignore the heady scent of her perfume. It was a shock. Not her demand—which was almost laughably inconsequential—but the intensity of his relief that she hadn't got up and stormed through the door. Irrational though it sounded, it didn't matter that the marriage hadn't happened. She already felt like his wife. And, having got so far, he wasn't about to lose her now.

Letting her win this particular battle was unimportant in the scheme of things. It certainly didn't mean that he was about to give her power over anything else—like his feelings, for example. Besides, he had other, more effective ways to remind her that he was in charge.

He raised his shoulders dismissively. 'Okay.

I'm happy for you to do that.' His eyes locked on to hers. 'Just as I'm sure *you're* happy to sign the prenuptial agreement I sent over.'

Turning, he picked a laminated folder up from the table behind the sofa and held it out to her.

'I take it you've read it?'

Margot nodded. Her heart began to thump against her chest.

He had emailed it over last night, and she'd gone over it twice. It contained no surprises. But it still jarred, though—stung, actually—the fact that ten years ago she had taken him at his word, whereas now he was demanding that she make no claim on his estate.

Her lips tightened. 'Yes, I've read it. There don't seem to be any problems.'

Aside from the small, incontrovertible fact that she was bartering herself to a man she had once loved without restraint, and with a hope she now found inconceivable.

Suddenly she just wanted to sign the damned thing and be gone. To be anywhere that Max wasn't.

She reached into her bag, but he was too fast for her.

'Here—use mine.'

He was holding out a black and gold fountain pen. It was identical to the one her grandfather used, and just for a moment she thought she might be sick. But, swallowing the metallic taste in her mouth, she took the pen from his fingers with what she hoped was an expression of pure indifference and, flipping through the document to the last page, carelessly scrawled her signature next to his, doing the same again seconds later on the other copy.

Misery snaked over her skin, but she wasn't about to let Max know how much she was hurting. He might hold all the cards, but there was some small satisfaction to be had from not acknowledging that fact—particularly to him.

Only suddenly that wasn't enough. Suddenly she didn't just want to hide her pain, she wanted to hurt him as he had hurt her. Laying the pen carefully on top of the paper, she looked up and deliberately fixed her gaze on his maddeningly handsome face.

'One last thing. Just so we're clear, this marriage is a business arrangement. Sex—' she punched the word towards him '—is not and is never going to be part of the deal. Whatever physical relationship we had, it happened a long time ago.'

A mocking smile tugged at his mouth. 'I wouldn't call twenty-four hours a long time.'

Mortified, she felt the air thump out of her lungs. How she regretted that kiss—or if not the kiss then the treacherous weakness of the body that had allowed it to happen.

'That was just curiosity,' she said quickly, trying to sound as if she meant it, as though only a fraction of her mind was on him.

'I just wanted a taste—you know, an *amuse bouche*. See if the menu was still worth sampling.' She was aware that her cheeks were flushed, that her voice was shaking ever so slightly, but she forced herself to hold his gaze. 'Only I guess I've grown up a lot. Had a bit more experience...tried different flavours. I know some couples go for that "sex with the ex" thing, but I'm going to pass on it.'

She could hardly believe the words that were coming out of her mouth. It felt unreal, talking that way, and to Max in particular, but she knew that she had his attention. For a moment she held her breath, waiting for his reaction, already anticipating his fury. But his face didn't change, and when finally he spoke his voice was as expressionless as his unblinking eyes.

'Of course you are—and now, unfortunately, I have another meeting scheduled. I hope you enjoyed your lunch...'

Gazing up at him, it took a moment for his words to sink in, and then, as they did, she realised with a rush of embarrassment that he was waiting politely and patiently for her to leave.

* * *

Back in her car, it took several minutes of deep breathing before her hands stopped shaking and she could start the engine. Pulling out into the late-afternoon traffic, she could feel questions pawing at her brain like a pack of dogs with a bone. Why had he acted like that? Why hadn't he thrown her remark back in her face?

Leaning back against the smooth leather seat, she rested her arm against the doorframe, and gnawed distractedly at her thumbnail.

Even at the most basic level her words would have been insulting to any man. But to Max it had been personal. So why had he deliberately chosen not to respond?

She pressed her thumb against the corner of her mouth. It was probably just another attempt to belittle her. Or maybe he was trying to mess with her head so that she'd end up with all these unanswerable questions swamping her brain. Or—

An icy shiver slipped down her spine, and she groaned softly.

Or maybe he just hadn't believed her.

And, really, why would he? When she didn't even believe herself?

Remembering the moment when he'd pressed his mouth to hers—the all-encompassing heat of that kiss and the way her body had surrendered to his—she felt heat flare low in her pelvis…

The blast of a horn burst into her thoughts, and she watched dully as a taxi surged past her, the driver gesticulating and shouting abuse into the warm, sticky air.

Her arms felt like jelly, and with an effort she indicated left, out of the city.

She was such a fool! Instead of puncturing his pride, her stupid denial had merely drawn attention to the terrible, humiliating truth. That she still wanted him with an intensity that was beyond her conscious control. But, terrible though it was to have betrayed herself like that, what was far worse was the private but equally devastating realisation that she couldn't imagine a time when that humiliating fact would ever change.

CHAPTER FIVE

RESTING HER HANDS against the edge of the balcony adjoining her hotel bedroom, Margot gazed out across the Indian Ocean, her brown eyes narrowing against the glare of morning sunlight, the thin silk of her robe lifting in the warm breeze coming off the water.

In just over five hours she would be Mrs Max Montigny—even just thinking that sentence made her feel dizzy. Or maybe that was the adrenaline. Her muscles clamped tighter. Either way, everything had all happened with such surreal speed that none of it felt real, and the sense of unreality was only being exacerbated by her idyllic surroundings.

Her gaze drifted back inland. The view from her hotel room was pure fantasy. A castaway island of palm-tree-framed beaches fusing with a dreamy turquoise sea. But there was a wildness to its beauty too, so that it was easy to feel you were the first person ever to leave your meandering footprints in the powdery white sands.

Raising a hand to block out the sun, she squinted down the beach. Perhaps not quite the first person. A figure was moving effortlessly across the dunes, covering the distance with impressive speed.

Wearing a black vest and shorts, his tanned skin gleaming like polished wood in the sunlight, Max was returning from his morning run. He moved with a focus and steadiness that in turn steadied *her*, so that some of her tension ebbed away.

Even from a distance, and with the sun in her eyes, his body looked just as spectacular as she remembered it—lean and sculptured and powerful. Her eyes lingered greedily on the striped bands of his taut, abdominal muscles before dropping to where the V of his obliques met the sagittal line of fine dark hair in the centre of his stomach.

He was so perfect, so tempting. An intoxicating blend of strength and beauty that made her feel weak with desire. Her mouth twisted. Not that she'd given in to temptation again. But being around Max again was not just unsettling physically, it was messing with her head too—dredging up memories, making her question the life she was living, the choices she'd made.

Over the last few years boyfriends had come and gone, but none had lasted, and that was completely understandable. Running the House of Duvernay was most definitely not a nine-to-five job, so her personal life had by necessity taken a back seat to her professional one, and she'd been grateful it had, for she hadn't been ready or willing to get too involved, to get hurt again, to *feel*.

Or rather she'd been scared not of feeling something but of never feeling *as much* for anyone as she'd felt for Max.

She bit her lip. Even now she could remember it—the stunned realisation, part-fear, part-euphoria that he had chosen *her*, wanted *her*.

Her stomach clenched. No, not her. Her money.

Breathing out, she gazed at the moving figure.

If only she could go back to that time—back to when she'd believed that he wanted her for herself. Her heart gave a twitch of irritation. And do what? Let her stupid, treacherous body betray her again?

She glanced back at Max, her eyes tracking his progress. The sun was already high overhead, but he seemed immune to the heat of its rays. He was running—no, make that sprinting—effortlessly across the sand, as though he was training for some elite military unit.

And then, as though he'd crossed an imaginary finishing line, he pulled up sharply, his legs slowing to a jog, then to a walk as he glanced down at his watch.

Her pulse was racing as hard as if she too had just run the length of the beach, and then her breath stalled in her throat as she watched him reach into the pocket of his shorts and pull out his phone.

She felt her eyes narrow. Surely today of all days he might have stopped working. But it was pointless getting angry about it. After all, it wasn't as though this marriage was anything other than a business arrangement for either of them.

Although, thanks to Max's extensive and careful preparations, nobody except the two of them would ever know that it wasn't real. Not only had he organised the paperwork and arranged the venue, he had sorted out the food, the flowers, and flown out a team of stylists to oversee everything on site. And everything was spot-on.

All she'd had to think about was the dress…

A light breeze lifted her hair in front of her face and, pushing it aside, she felt her pulse dip. Given that she was only marrying Max to save her business, it really shouldn't matter what she wore. But, to her surprise, her wedding gown still felt like more than just a dress to her.

Staring up at the cloudless sky, she let the sun warm her face. Back in Paris, feeling harried by the pace of his arrangements, she had considered choosing an off-the-peg dress from one of the big department stores. It had been a childish impulse, really—another meaningless attempt to prove how little she cared about him and their phony wedding.

But in the end she hadn't been able to bring herself to do it. And it hadn't just been because of the risk that somebody might spot her browsing the rails and leak it to the media.

Lowering her head, she drew in a deep breath. She was a Duvernay, and in her family's history weddings were not just celebrations but life-impacting events, defined not just by who you married but what you wore.

Her grandmother's dress had been spectacular. A fairy tale confection with metres of tulle and millions of hand-sewn pearls. It had taken fifty seamstresses nearly three months to create.

In contrast, her mother had recycled the simple knee-length tulle-skirted dress that she'd worn for her eighteenth birthday party.

Each had known instinctively what she wanted to wear to marry the man she had chosen to be her husband. Only where did that leave her? She was marrying a man she didn't love, out of necessity. What exactly was the dress code for a marriage of convenience?

Despite the heat of the sun, Margot shivered.

It didn't help that she was being forced to do something she'd actually dreamed of doing. Ten years ago she had been happily imagining a wedding day in the future. Only Max had been more than just her groom—he'd been the air she breathed, the gravitational pull of her world.

For a second she braced herself against the pain, fingers tightening against the balustrade. But that had been then. In the present, this wedding wasn't about Max. Just like the rest of her life, it was about creating an illusion.

She needed her grandfather to accept her sudden decision to get married. Actually, she wanted him to be happy about it. Only with the speed and secrecy of the arrangements so closely mirroring his daughter's elopement, she knew that the only way to make that happen was by staging the perfect wedding.

And, no matter how little time there had been, Max Montigny's wife would *never* wear a department store dress. Her gown, just like her ring, would have to look the part. As her groom undoubtedly would.

Max was still talking on his phone, his handsome face relaxed and unguarded, and something about his expression made her heart contract—for she could still remember just how heavenly it had felt to be the object of that gaze.

Her fingers trembled against the smooth wood

as she wondered what it would feel like if today was actually real, and instead of her money or her business, Max actually wanted her.

It was not the first time that thought had crossed her mind. In fact, it had been popping into her head with maddening regularity ever since she'd watched him walk out of her board-room that first day. But thinking it could ever happen would require an almost childlike level of imagination, and she was done with building castles in the air. The only castle she cared about now was her family home.

She needed to focus on the facts—which were that Max might be in control of her business, but she was in control of everything else. And that included how she chose to respond to him. All she had to do was stay cool and detached and civil and their marriage would hopefully be ci-vilised too.

Glancing down at Max's sweat-slicked skin, she licked her lips. That might be easier in the-ory than in practice. Although Max wasn't quite the barbarian she'd accused him of being, he was still the least civilised person she'd ever met, seemingly untroubled by blackmail and extor-tion.

However, even from the short amount of time they'd spent discussing his plans for Duvernay, she had to admit that he'd actually been modest when he'd said he had a head for business. He was smart, quick and creative—and, although he had an innate authority that reminded her of her grandfather, he was also surprisingly willing to listen to his staff. And even more surprisingly to her.

She had expected to be swept aside, but instead, at his suggestion, they would be working together as co-CEOs, his argument being that having 'two in the box' was better than one.

If only their marriage could be as equable and as close, she thought wistfully.

At that moment, almost as if he could hear her thoughts, Max turned and stared fixedly across the beach towards her balcony.

Her pulse jumped. Hot-cheeked, horrified that she had been discovered in such a blatant act of voyeurism, she turned her face away from the magnetic pull of his gaze and inched back into her room.

Her skin was prickling. *Oh, how was she going to do this?* She couldn't even face him at a distance and from the safety of her hotel room. How was she going to stand opposite him and repeat vows neither of them believed to be true?

If only there was another way…

But there wasn't.

Duvernay's problems were not going to just disappear, and that was why she was here and why she was going to go through with this marriage.

A knock on the door broke into her thoughts and, grateful for the interruption, she tightened her wrap. The time for thinking was over. Now she needed to get ready for her wedding.

Three hours later she was standing nervously in front of the mirror, gazing at her reflection. The transformation was complete.

'You look beautiful.'

Her eyes darted gratefully to Camille Feuillet, friend and premier couturier from her favourite fashion house, who had flown out from Paris late last night. She had known the older woman ever since she was a gauche teenager, struggling with shyness and a famous mother. Camille had helped her find a style, and she was the one person she'd trusted to design a dress for her wedding day.

'It's lovely,' she said slowly. 'Camille, you are so clever. I never dreamed that it would look like this—that I could look like this.'

She had expected to feel different, but this was like alchemy. The dress was exquisite—and romantic. Camille had insisted on finishing the final details herself, hand-embroidering Margot and Max's initials into the beautiful, intricate floral lace veil.

Margot felt suddenly shy. Thanks to the

woman standing beside her she would not only be able to convince her family and the world's media that she was marrying the love of her life, she would be able to do so feeling good about herself—just like a real bride.

'Thank you, Camille,' she said softly.

'You are so welcome.' Camille smiled, and then her face creased and she brushed a hand against her eyes. 'I promised myself I wouldn't cry but I can't help it. You just look so lovely.'

'More like lucky!' Despite the ache in her chest, the smile she gave the other woman was genuine. Camille had made her a wedding dress of heart-stopping beauty. It wasn't her fault the wedding itself was a sham of what it might have been.

'You've given me so much help and inspiration. I couldn't have done it without you, so thank you. And thank you for coming all this way. I know how busy you are—'

'It was my pleasure.' Camille hesitated, and then, glancing over at Margot, she giggled. 'Besides, I think this might be the one time your extremely cool fiancé actually gets a little hot under the collar, and I wouldn't want to miss that for anything.'

Margot nodded. Her smile didn't falter, but she felt her pulse quiver. No doubt most grooms *did* get emotional, seeing their bride, but then most grooms hadn't blackmailed their bride down the aisle. And Max didn't *do* emotion—or at least not the romantic, helpless kind of emotion that Camille was talking about.

Instead, he was fine-tuned for winning.

Remembering the dark, calculating glitter in his eyes when he'd kissed her in the boardroom, she knew that his desire was as cold and controlled as his heart. Whatever Max was feeling and thinking right now, she would lay odds that it had more to do with his business than his forthcoming nuptials.

'Are you ready?'

Camille's voice broke into her thoughts and, steadying her breathing, she turned and nodded. Then, pinching the edges of the veil between her fingers, she lowered it carefully over her face and walked slowly towards the door and her future.

On the other side of the hotel, his dark suit a contrast to the bleached boards of the chapel, Max Montigny stared down at his phone, his fingers hovering over the keyboard.

He was standing slightly apart from the priest, and the two elderly estate workers who had been carefully chosen by his security team to act as witnesses for the wedding were waiting patiently behind him, but he was barely aware of them, or of his surroundings.

Not the sun that had drained the colour out of the sky, or the tiny open-sided chapel that was smothered in white frangipani flowers. All his concentration was fixed on his phone.

He read the message on the screen, deleted a few words, retyped them and then finally deleted them all.

Switching the phone to 'silent', he dropped it in his pocket. It had taken him nearly ten years to get to this point, and he wasn't about to tempt fate with an unnecessary and premature text. Soon enough Margot would be wearing his ring, and then the whole world would be able to see that Max Montigny was the equal of the Duvernays.

He breathed in sharply. The thought of Margot finally becoming Mrs Montigny was dizzying. Bracing his shoulders, he gazed at the ocean. If only he could steady his breathing… But it was impossible to do so, for every time he inhaled, the warm, fragrant air reminded him of the perfume Margot wore.

It was driving him crazy. Not just the fact that the scent of her seemed to be following him everywhere, but the way it conjured up the memory of her brown-eyed challenge in his hotel room.

'*I just wanted a taste...you know, an* amuse bouche. *See if the menu was still worth sampling. I know some couples go for that "sex with the ex" thing, but I'm going to pass.*'

He'd known she was lying, but somehow that only made her claim more maddening—and frustrating.

Ignoring the pulse beating in his groin, he straightened his cuffs and turned towards the priest and the witnesses, nodding in acknowledgement. From years of keeping his own counsel he knew that the expression on his face gave nothing away—not even a hint as to the thoughts twisting through his head—and the thought calmed him. Revealing emotion—*feeling* emotion—was an act of self-destruction, a handing over of power to the person most equipped to hurt you the most.

And that was particularly true of the woman he was about to marry.

He let out a slow, unsteady breath. What amazed him was that he'd actually got this far. Back in France when Margot had given in to his demands, he had been too busy struggling with the various emotions produced by seeing her again to register the full consequences of his proposal.

It had been an act of impulse and pride— for, much as he'd moved on with his life, a part of him had never forgotten or forgiven her for throwing his proposal back in his face, just as he himself had been thrown off the Duvernay estate.

Now, though, impulse would become legal fact—a contract only dissolvable by law. In less than an hour Margot would be his wife, and that thought blew his mind. Or it would have done if he hadn't chosen that particular moment to look up.

His heart gave a lurch and his fingers tightened involuntarily as he watched Margot step tentatively into the chapel, her wary brown gaze resting on his face as she approached him.

Behind him, he heard someone—the priest, probably—clear his throat. There was a flurry of activity and he knew that he should turn round, that he needed to turn round in order for the ceremony to start. But he couldn't look away. His eyes were beyond his control, following her hungrily, pulled by some inexorable force, like twin tides dragged by the luminous pale loveliness of a new moon.

He felt his heart slam against his ribcage, his eyes taking in every detail as she took another step towards him—and then stopped. A hush like a held breath had fallen over the chapel, and even the ocean's waves seemed to be silent, as though their ceaseless motion had been stilled by the presence of such flawless beauty.

She looked exquisite. Beneath the veil her long blonde hair was scooped into some kind of low bun, her bare shoulders were gleaming in the sunlight, and her dress...

His gaze travelled over the delicate lace of her bodice to the gently flaring skirt. He had expected her to look lovely—what bride didn't? But Margot was more than just beautiful. She had always been more than just beautiful. She was a mystery that he'd obsessively wanted to solve, that had always been just beyond his reach.

Until now.

And so, ignoring tradition, he walked towards her and held out his hand.

The service was short and to the point. Speaking the vows, and listening to Margot repeat the familiar promises of love and loyalty in her soft, unwavering voice, he couldn't actually believe that it was happening. And yet here he was, sliding the band of diamonds set in gold onto her finger, and she was pushing a plain gold band onto his.

Lifting her veil, he watched the pupils of her eyes widen in the shade of the chapel. The certificate they would sign in a moment would be tangible evidence that finally he had proved her and her family wrong. That was why he was here, and he should be feeling relief, satisfaction, triumph… And yet he felt tense, almost restless, as though there was something more… something more important than retribution only he wasn't sure what it was.

His gaze shifted, slid upwards to her eyes, and he took a deep breath, confounded by the conflict he saw there. It reminded him of that first winter he and his mother had moved to Paris, struggling with the sudden loss of their old life and with feelings he hadn't understood.

He'd felt so young and helpless, so lost and alone, so stripped of all defences, and the thought that Margot should be feeling like that now resonated inside him, so that suddenly his stomach was churning, his breath jamming in his throat.

His hand twitched and he almost reached out, as any human would, instinctively wanting to comfort her. But to have done so would have been clumsy—inappropriate, somehow.

Quickly, he reminded himself that the only way this marriage would work would be to keep memories and emotions out of it. She had agreed to become his wife and he didn't owe her any gentleness. He could simply have sat back and watched her business collapse, but instead he had given her and her family a way out from financial ruin and public humiliation.

It might not be the marriage she wanted, to the man she wanted, but as far as he was concerned she had got more than she deserved.

'Margot and Max, you have expressed your love to one another through the commitment and promises you have made, and celebrated your union with the giving and receiving of rings.' The priest smiled.

It was just words, Margot told herself nervously.

But, hearing the priest talk about love and commitment, she felt her heart start to pound. Glancing down at her hand, Margot stared at the diamond band nestling against her engagement ring. It was breathtakingly beautiful. Elegant. Timeless. And it wasn't just the ring. Everything—the sun-soaked setting, the lush, fragrant flowers, the smiling priest, even Max himself— was so perfect it was impossible to resist.

Her pulse gave a leap like a startled deer.

Especially Max.

He was close enough that she could differentiate between the heat of his body and the warmth of the spice-warm air.

Dry-mouthed, she stared at him, her eyes fluttering helplessly over the man standing beside her, her gaze drawn to his face. Not because he was now her husband, but because he was and would always be her magnetic north, and the pull between them was beyond any kind of rational thought.

Particularly when he looked so devastating.

The dark fabric of his suit fitted him like a second skin, and the pure, brilliant whiteness of his shirt perfectly offset his compelling eyes and *café crème* colouring. In the shade of the chapel his features looked as though they might have been cast from bronze.

He was the perfect groom in every way, and just for a moment she couldn't help herself. All the promises she'd made to herself earlier that morning were overridden, and she let herself imagine what it would be like if this was a marriage of love and Max simply wanted *her*.

That thought was still uppermost in her mind as the priest looked across and, smiling again at both of them, said quietly, 'You are no longer simply partners and best friends. Today you have chosen to be joined in marriage. Therefore, it is my pleasure to pronounce you husband and wife. Max, you may now kiss your bride!'

Max felt a jolt pass through his body. So that was it. It was over—finished. Done.

Or maybe it was just beginning.

His breath seemed to tear his throat as he looked into Margot's eyes. Something was happening in them. They held an expression half-startled, half-spellbound.

And then he realised why.

He wasn't sure of how or when it had happened but he was holding her, his arm curving around her back so that she was pressed against his body.

He stared down at her, a flutter of heat side-winding over his skin. Her lips were the same colour as rose petals, her mouth a curving pink bow that he knew tasted as good as it looked. Kissing her was part of the ceremony. But after what she'd said to him in his hotel it felt more like a dare. A chance to raise the stakes. A challenge he could not walk away from.

He wanted to prove her wrong—to show her and everyone watching that she couldn't resist him. And, lowering his head, he let his mouth brush against hers. It was more of a graze than a kiss, fleeting and feather-light. But even as he lifted his head he felt his stomach flip. She stared up at him in silence, her gaze finding something, needing something...

And, looking down into her wide, unguarded brown eyes, he felt a rush of possessive desire as swift and unstoppable as white water rapids.

Finally, she was his wife.

His.

Pulling her soft body closer, her slid a finger under her chin and tipped her head up. His heart was pounding and the air was tightening around them as he studied her face. And then he was kissing her hungrily, one hand wrapping around her waist, the other pushing through her hair, anchoring her against him.

Margot felt the ground tip beneath her feet.

Grabbing at his jacket, she clutched at the smooth fabric as his tongue parted her lips. And then she was falling…falling back in time…her body responding unquestioningly, willingly, to the power and heat of his mouth.

Around her the world was spinning faster and faster, like a ride at the funfair. She felt giddy and clumsy and boneless. All she could do was cling on tight to the one solid object she could find. And, leaning into Max's hard, muscular body, she closed her eyes.

And suddenly there was only Max. His mouth, his hands, the warm density of his chest. She wanted him, and she had no conscious thought or physical wish to hold back, to do anything but open her body to his.

But even as the taste of him filled her mouth she felt his body tense, and then he was breaking the kiss, and instead of his pulse beating through her veins like a metronome she could hear the tranquil sound of nearby waves washing onto the beach.

Dazedly she looked up at him, pressing her hand against his chest to steady herself. But only for a second.

She felt her body stiffen, and a damp stickiness began creeping over her skin. Only it had nothing to do with the balmy subtropical heat and everything to do with the cool, appraising look in his eyes.

Her limbs felt as if they were made of wood.

Had she learnt nothing from the past?

Ten years ago Max had used other such kisses to seduce her, to fool her into believing his lies. This time, though, he didn't need to fool her. It was the priest and the witnesses he needed to convince, so that they would see what he wanted them to see. Not an act of coercion or revenge, but two people declaring their love for one another.

And clearly it had worked.

She felt her stomach plunge as the priest stepped forward, his gentle face creased in a smile of wonder and approval. 'You have kissed many times, I'm sure. But today your kiss means so much more. It has sealed your marriage. Today, your kiss is a promise.'

Max looked over at her, his eyes glinting as

they swept over the flush that she knew was colouring her cheekbones.

'Yes, it is,' he said slowly. 'One I fully intend
to keep.'

They were signing the register. Margot felt as
though she was sleepwalking. Posing above the
heavy leather-bound book, pen in hand, she
smiled for the photographer, trying her hardest
to look like the radiant bride that her grandfather
and brother would be expecting to see.

There was confetti, champagne and congrat-
ulations. By the time they were walking back
to the hotel Margot's mouth was aching with
the effort of smiling and she felt exhausted, but
also relieved, for now that it was done there was
no more need to agonise over whether she was
doing the right thing.

She was Margot Montigny now. And she knew
that her grandfather and Louis would accept her
marriage. For the first time since Emile had
dropped his bombshell the burden she was carrying felt lighter. Now all she wanted to do was get
back to France and break the news to her family.

Stomach swooping downwards, she stepped
unthinkingly into the waiting limousine. And
then, as the doors closed and the sleek black car
began to move forward, she felt a sharp dart of
apprehension.

Frowning, she turned to Max. 'Where are we going? I thought we were eating at the hotel.'

His handsome face looked relaxed, and the colour of his eyes was indistinguishable in the cool, shaded interior of the car. 'It's a surprise,' he said softly.

Her heart thumped clumsily against her ribs. 'I don't like surprises.'

His eyes rested on her face, and something about the steady calmness of his gaze unnerved her more than his words.

'Is that right? I thought all women liked surprises.'

She glared at him. 'Flattering though it is to be compared to every other female on the planet, I would rather just stick to the plan. The plan we agreed on.'

Something flared in his eyes. 'We just got married. Can't I be just a little bit romantic?'

Ignoring the prickle of heat in her cheeks, Margot stared at him. 'Not in my experience— no. Besides, we both know this isn't about romance, so stop pretending it is and take me back to the hotel.'

His gaze was steady on her face. 'That's not going to happen.'

She shook her head. 'Oh, yes, it is. You said we would eat and then fly home.'

'I did, didn't I?'

He shifted in his seat, and something in the casual way he leaned back against the leather made a fog of panic swirl up inside of her.

'So what's changed?' She glowered at him.

He shrugged, but his eyes on hers were curiously intent. '*You* have, baby. Before you were just a woman—now you're my wife.'

Her heart contracted. 'I know I'm your wife,' she said mutinously. 'But I don't see why that means we can't eat at the hotel. Or not eat at all.' She held his gaze. 'I'd be happy to fly home now.'

'And miss our honeymoon?' he said softly. 'What would people think? And I know how much you care about what people think, Margot.'

The blood drained from her face. Something cold and clammy was inching down her spine. 'No, that's not what we agreed, Max.' Her voice was a whisper now. 'You can't do that—'

'And yet I am.' His gaze swept over her face. 'Don't worry. It's no trouble. You see, I have a house here. Just along the coast. And that's where we're going to spend the next two weeks. Just the two of us. What could be more romantic than that?'

CHAPTER SIX

THE DRIVE TO the house passed quickly and silently.

For Margot, silence was the only possible option. Pressed into the corner of the car, she was just too angry to speak. But inside her head angry accusations were whirling around like a flock of seabirds.

How dared he do this?

How dared he unilaterally change their plans? Ignore everything that they'd agreed, trample over her feelings and wishes?

She'd agreed to marry him on one condition—that she could speak to her family before rumours of their wedding became public knowledge. It was the only condition she'd set, and even though she was doing everything he'd asked he still hadn't managed to do that one thing for her.

Her jaw clenched painfully. How could she be so gullible? All that rubbish about being happy to tell her grandfather in person, letting her believe that they were going to fly back to France, when all the time he'd just been pretending so that he could do what he'd said he'd wanted to do right at the start—watch her family suffer.

She glared at him, her cheeks flushing with colour. He was selfish, thoughtless and utterly untrustworthy.

Her fingers curled into the fabric of her dress. All her life it had been the same, the people who were supposed to love her had just done what they wanted, put their needs above hers, and then expected her to put up with it.

No, not just put up with it, she thought savagely. They actually expected her to smile in public while in private they turned her world upside down.

But then selflessness was not part of her family's DNA. Or apparently her new husband's.

Beside her, Max stretched out his legs—a man without a care in the world. A man who was apparently either oblivious to or unconcerned by her silence.

She clenched her teeth. It wasn't that she'd expected him to be thoughtful. Given that he was blackmailing her into marrying him that would have been insane. But surely the whole point of this stupid arranged marriage was that there were rules…boundaries. They'd made an agreement and now Max had broken it.

Her hands tightened in her lap. It wasn't the unfairness of his actions that was so upsetting. Nor did she really care about ego. This was about her grandfather and her brother, and how they would feel when they woke up tomorrow and discovered that she'd sneaked off behind their backs to get married.

Her heart contracted. There was no way she could get in touch with her grandfather. She couldn't risk waking him with news like that— not when his health was so precarious. And while she *could* try ringing Louis…really, what would be the point? It was the last night of his holiday. He was probably out celebrating and having fun with his friends. If she spoke to him now it would ruin everything.

Her heart gave an angry thump.

If Max had done what he'd agreed they'd do, and they had flown back to France, she would have been able to make things right.

She'd had it all planned. They would go straight to the chateau and Max would wait downstairs while she took breakfast up to her grandfather. His favourite breakfast: *café au lait* and eggs benedict—a legacy of his time in America—but using a slice of *tartine* instead of muffins. Then she would sit on the chair beside his bed and take as long as was necessary to reassure him that she hadn't turned into her mother.

It wouldn't be easy, but she knew that she would make him understand. And once he was dressed and composed they would go downstairs together, and everything would be fine.

She swallowed. Now, though, Max had made that moment impossible. Now her grandfather would wake to the news headlines that his beloved and utterly reliable granddaughter had been lying to his face and had eloped.

He would be heartbroken. And there was no doubt in her mind that, whatever he'd just told her about wanting to surprise her, that had been Max's intention all along.

'I know how much you care about what people think, Margot.'

Her skin felt hot, her cheeks burning with humiliation that she should have been so stupid as to trust him. Stiff, angry words were bubbling in her throat and she turned towards him, her eyes seeking his in the cool darkness of the limo's interior.

But before she could open her mouth to unleash her fury she felt the car start to slow and realised that they had arrived at Max's house.

She watched him step out into the sunshine, and then somehow she was taking his hand. There was a small round of applause and, glancing up, she saw that they were not alone. A group of people—presumably Max's staff—all wearing white polo shirts and cream-coloured shorts were standing in two lines on either side of the stairway leading up to the house, their friendly faces beaming down at her.

But it was not their smiles or even the brightness of the sun that made her blink. It was the building behind them.

Her heart bumped against her ribs. Theoretically, she knew the extent of Max's wealth. But, gazing up at the beautiful white modernist villa, she finally understood just how hard he must have worked, and despite the fury simmering inside her she couldn't stop herself from admiring the way he had managed to create this life for himself.

Was it really so surprising, though? Even when she'd first met him it had been clear that Max was no average employee. It hadn't been just his good looks that had made him stand out from everybody else. He'd been bright, focused, creative and exceptionally determined.

Her mouth twisted.

No doubt the same ruthless determination that had made him such a successful businessman made it equally easy for him to disrespect her wishes. She needed to remember that the next time she felt like admiring him.

Inside the villa the decor was modern, almost austere, and only a subtle change in flooring from bleached wood to the palest pink marble signalled the transition between inside and out. But even if the change had been signposted with flashing neon lights she would barely have noticed the difference, for her attention was fixed on the terrace where, beside the bluest pool she had ever seen, a beautiful glass table was set for two beneath a gleaming white sail-like canopy.

Gazing past the table to the ocean beyond, Margot swallowed. She had forgotten all about eating, and she was simmering with so much suppressed rage that she'd completely lost her appetite anyway. But this was her 'wedding breakfast', and of course to accompany the meal there would be—

'Champagne, darling?'

Max stepped forward, his eyes resting on her face, the irises so startlingly blue and green that she had a sudden vivid flashback to the first time they'd met, and how it hadn't felt real. Not just the dual colours of his gaze, but the fact that he was *there*, in her kitchen, this extraordinary, arrestingly beautiful man, talking and laughing and smiling...

Her spine stiffened. And now he was smiling at her again. Only not as a dangerously handsome stranger, but as her dangerously handsome, *self-serving* husband.

'I chose it especially,' he said softly. Leaning forward, he twisted the bottle towards her so that she could see the label. 'It's the Duvernay Grand Cru from the year we first met.'

Her lips curved into a stiff smile as she took the brimming glass. 'How considerate of you,' she said tightly.

There was a pulsing silence, and then he gently tapped his glass against hers.

'You see—it's almost like your family are already here, giving us their blessing.' His mocking gaze flickered over her face. 'And, really, what better way could there be to mark the start of *our* married life than a glass of champagne from *our* estate?'

She stared past him. 'Oh, I can think of one or two scenarios.'

He laughed. 'Why do I get the feeling that all of them involve me being in some kind of mortal peril?'

Shaking his head, he lounged back against his seat.

'I meant what I said in the chapel, Margot. As of now, you're my wife. For better, for worse… for richer, for poorer.' He gave a slow smile. 'Or, given our particular agreement, maybe that should be for poorer, for richer.'

For a moment she considered throwing the contents of her glass in his face, but just then one of his staff stepped forward with a selection of canapés, and instead she took a mouthful of champagne.

It was a good year, she thought dispassionately. An almost perfect balance of citrus and cream, with a just a hint of raspberry.

Her muscles tightened. Her grandfather had always said that a great champagne was like a love potion, but it would have to be a remarkable vintage indeed for her to forget that their marriage was a business merger in everything but name. And that Max was a total snake in the grass.

Through a combination of polite, if a little stilted, conversation and carefully timed smiles, she managed to get through the meal. Then the still smiling staff started to melt away, and finally they were alone.

Instantly she pushed her untouched cup of coffee away, her fingers twitching against the table-top.

Max stared at her with a mixture of mockery and resignation. 'The monsoon season is over for this year,' he said softly, lowering his gaze so that his eyes were suddenly in shadow. 'And yet I sense a storm is brewing.'

'Damn right it is.' Instantly her bottled-up resentment rose to the surface, like the bubbles in her family's legendary champagne. 'If you think I'm staying here for two weeks with you, acting out some pantomime of a honeymoon, then you must be insane. We had a deal. I have kept my side of that deal, and I expect you to keep yours. So, unless you have a reason for changing our plans other than sheer bloody-mindedness, I suggest you get hold of your pilot and tell him that we will be leaving for France tonight.'

'Or what? Are you going to swim home?'

She glared at him. 'If it means getting away from you, then, yes.'

He didn't reply—just stared at her so intently and for so long that she wanted to scream. And then finally, in a gesture that seemed designed solely to aggravate her, he shrugged carelessly.

Margot glanced at him helplessly. She felt as though she would burst with rage. Was that the sum total of his response? Was that seriously supposed to be some kind of answer?

'What does that mean?' she snapped. She could hear her overstretched nerves vibrating in her voice, but she didn't care any more. 'You're not in some *nouvelle vague* film, Max. This is real life. My life. And I am your wife—legally, at least—so could you at least do me the courtesy of actually saying something?'

Raising an eyebrow, seemingly unperturbed by either her words or her tone, he gazed at her impassively. 'Okay—it means that any deal we made most certainly did *not* include you flouncing off to the airport to catch the first flight home after we'd exchanged our wedding vows.'

His expression didn't shift, but she felt a sudden rise in tension as she mimicked his tone. 'Well, *any deal we made* also didn't include you and me building sandcastles for two weeks.' She glared at him. 'I mean, what exactly do you think we're going to spend our honeymoon doing?'

There was a tiny quivering pause, just long enough for her to realise the full, horrifying idiocy of what she'd said, and then the air seemed to ripple around her as her words continued to echo into the sudden silence.

What she had been trying to say was that as theirs wasn't a regular kind of marriage, their honeymoon was hardly going to be all moonlight walks and long afternoons in bed.

Only it hadn't sounded the way she'd intended. In fact it couldn't have sounded any worse.

Her throat felt suddenly scratchy and dry as, leaning forward, he gave her an infuriating smile.

'Oh, I expect we could probably think of something to pass the time...'

She wanted to deny it. But the trouble was, he was right—and, no matter how much she wanted it to be otherwise, it didn't change the fact that her body still ached for the wordless, exquisite satisfaction that he alone had given her.

Rigid with mortification, her cheeks flooded with colour, she glanced past him, cursing herself, cursing him, and cursing her father for putting her in this impossible position.

If only she could just flick a switch so that she could stop feeling like this. If only it was just thinking. If only she could just separate her body from her brain. But as her mind filled with images of her and Max moving in blurred slow motion she felt her breath quicken.

Suddenly her heart was pounding, and she could almost taste the adrenalin. She felt like a gladiator, waiting outside the arena, poised and ready for combat. Only this time it was herself she was fighting. Her desire for Max was dangerous and, as she knew from experience, the kind of passion they shared came at a price. It trampled over your pride, crushed your dreams and cleaved your heart in two.

Ignoring the clamouring demands of her body, she lifted her chin. 'I know we could. But that doesn't mean that we should.' She swallowed, struggling to find the words that would stop her feeling, stop her needing. 'So if that's why you broke our agreement then I'm sorry to disappoint you, but unlike you I have principles.'

His eyes glittered and, sensing the anger unfurling beneath his apparently calm demeanour, she felt her stomach clench. But he had no right to feel angry. He hadn't been bullied and manipulated. He hadn't been made to perform like a puppet on a string.

She took a breath, desperate to divert the conversation to less dangerous territory. 'Besides, in case you've forgotten, you're supposed to be saving my business—and you can't do that if we're both here cavorting about on a beach!'

Her heartbeat scampered. Even now that Max was co-running Duvernay she still felt horribly responsible. She had already been worried about taking more time off work so soon after going to Monte Carlo, but she had been expecting to be gone for just a few days, not two weeks.

His lazy gaze didn't shift from her face, but the air felt suddenly fat with tension.

'Luckily for you, I can multitask,' he said coolly.

Max stared at her. He was good at multitasking, but right now he was struggling to hold on to his temper at the same time as trying to justify why just one kiss had overridden his meticulous and completely non-negotiable plan to return to France immediately after the wedding.

His temper wasn't improved by Margot insisting on talking about Duvernay. She was acting as if he was just some troubleshooter she'd hired to fix her damned business instead of her husband. And she had accused him of being un-romantic!

He gritted his teeth. Maybe they should have gone home. Everything had been in place. His private jet had been waiting on the runway and he had personally signed off on a carefully worded statement to the press about his sudden marriage to Margot Duvernay. All that there had been left to do was make a phone call—a call he had been wanting and waiting to make for so long—and then finally he would have been able to flaunt his new wife to the world.

Only as he'd brought his mouth down on hers and she'd leaned into him everything had changed.

Holding her body, feeling her frantic, un-guarded response, he had been engulfed by a raw and ferocious need that had blotted out all logical thought. There and then he'd decided that the rest of the world could wait. Finally Margot was his wife. She was his, and—for the foresee-able future, at least—he was not going to share her with anyone.

But he was not about to admit that out loud, and certainly not to Margot—particularly when all she seemed bothered about was her wretched business.

'I don't leave things to chance,' he said. 'I

have people reporting back to me and everything's running smoothly.' He lounged back in his chair, letting his long legs sprawl out in front of him. 'Why are you making this into such a big deal? You wanted traditional, and a honeymoon is a wedding tradition. I'm just ticking all the boxes,' he lied.

Margot looked at him resentfully. It was true that she had wanted to keep the wedding as traditional as possible, but only for the benefit of her grandfather and Louis. And she had never so much as hinted at having a honeymoon.

A honeymoon!

Her brain stumbled, tripping on a thought of just exactly how she and Max might spend their honeymoon. Sunlit hours passing into darkness, hands splaying against warm, damp skin, bodies shuddering, surrendering to one bone-dissolving climax after another—

Her heart was pounding.

'Then I suggest you untick them,' she said curtly.

His gaze didn't so much as flicker. 'I must say I'm a little surprised—I wasn't expecting wedding day nerves,' he said lazily. 'And there was I, thinking you were only marrying me for my money.'

She gave a humourless laugh. 'You're deluded.'

'And you're overreacting,' he said coolly.

'Overreacting?' She shook her head in disbelief. 'If you don't understand why I need to get back then you must be even more insensitive and self-serving than I thought.'

Her brown eyes narrowed.

'Perhaps you were raised by wolves. Or maybe you don't have any family,' she snarled. 'Or maybe, like every other unfortunate soul who crosses your path, they prefer to keep well clear of you. Frankly, I don't much care.'

Watching his features grow harder, she felt a quiver of unease. But so what if she'd offended him? If someone basically lied, and then lied again, why should she be nice about it?

She took a deep breath. 'But I do care about my family. You knew I wanted to tell to my grandfather in person. You knew it, and yet you completely ignored my wishes.'

He let his gaze rest on her accusing face. '*Your life. Your wishes.* You seem to be forgetting that this isn't just about you. It's about us. But then you never really got the hang of *us*, did you, Margot?'

Margot stared at him unsteadily, the air thumping out of her lungs. How was this her fault? He wasn't the one who'd been tricked and manipulated, lied to and misled.

Her body was quivering with anger and frustration. Was this how it was going to be? Every conversation filled with pitfalls and traps, like a game of snakes and ladders where a stray move or two could send them tumbling back into the past.

Suddenly her eyes felt hot, and she blinked frantically. She was not going to cry. She was not going to let him know that he could hurt her. But she also wasn't going to sit here and listen to his stupid, self-righteous accusations—not after everything he'd said and done to her.

'That's because there was no *us*, Max.' Her breathing jerked, for even as she said the words, a part of her was hoping he would deny them. But of course he didn't. He just continued to stare at her, his face expressionless, his eyes still and steady.

She cleared her throat. 'There was me, and there was you. We were different people. We wanted different things then, and we want different things now. Nothing's changed.'

His eyes lifted to hers. 'Except that now you're my wife,' he said slowly.

Mesmerised by the possessive note in his voice, she was suddenly holding her breath. And then almost immediately she felt a chill come over her body. Was she really that shallow? Surely this conversation encapsulated everything that had been wrong between them, and explained why their relationship could never be what it should. Sex acting as a substitute for tenderness and sensitivity? Aged nineteen, she hadn't really understood the difference, or maybe she'd thought it would be enough.

But now she did—and it wasn't.

'So what if I am?' she said, finally finding her voice. 'You've made it clear that I don't matter to you. You don't respect me or my feelings, or care about my opinions. And you sure as hell don't understand relationships. Or is this *really* what you think marriage is supposed to be like?'

She broke off, hating the emotion in her voice. Suddenly she couldn't bear it any more. There was no point in talking to him. Standing up, she took hold of her wedding ring and tugged it loose from her finger.

'Here—you can have this back. You see, it doesn't matter how many rings you give me, Max, or even how many bits of paper I sign, I will never truly belong to you.'

She tossed the ring onto the table and then, clutching the fabric of her skirt, she turned and walked stiffly towards the villa.

Somehow she found her way to her—their—bedroom. It was decorated in the same style as the rest of the house, all pale wood and neutral-coloured walls. Cool, contemporary, masculine.

Except the bed.

She gazed in stunned, wordless disbelief at the beautiful four-poster bed, a lump building in her

throat. On the other side of the room the doors
to the deck had been left open, and the canopy
of muslin above the bed was quivering in the
warm tropical breeze. Beneath the canopy, the
white sheets and pillows were strewn with the
palest pink and white petals. It was ludicrously,
perfectly romantic.

Her pulse was suddenly racing, and warmth
stole over her skin as, dazedly, she stepped closer
to the bed. Reaching down, she let her fingers
drift over the crisp white sheets. Kicking off her
shoes, she felt her heart contract. Everything
was such a mess.

Ten years ago this would have been everything she wanted, and she wished with an intensity that was painful that she could just forget
the past and—

And what? What exactly was she supposed to
do and feel now?

There were hundreds, maybe thousands of
books and blogs outlining wedding etiquette,
and probably even more devoted to achieving
a happy marriage. But what were the rules for
Max and Margot? The first time she had loved
him unconditionally and he had wanted her
money. Now he wanted her business and she
needed his financial support.

She felt suddenly close to tears again.

Being married to Max was just so much more

complex than she'd imagined it would be. In her head, she'd pictured something like her grandparents' marriage—traditional, formal. They had married young, not for love but for dynastic reasons. But despite that unpromising start they had grown to care for one another, and there had always been respect and trust. How were she and Max ever going to get to that stage?

Her body tensed, and she sensed that she was no longer alone. Somebody had come into the bedroom, and without turning she knew it was Max. She didn't have to see him. The connection between them was so intense she recognised him simply by the prickling heat creeping over her skin, and the way the compass point inside her began to quiver.

She couldn't help herself. Turning, she felt her body still as she watched him walk slowly towards her.

Don't come any closer, she thought, her breath catching in her throat.

'Why not?' he said softly, and her pulse began to race as she realised that without meaning to do so she must have spoken out loud.

'There's no reason for you to do so,' she said, flattening the emotion out of her voice. 'You've got the marriage licence and the share certificates, so you have everything you want.'

He stopped in front of her, and for one endless

moment they stared at each other, wide-eyed, their bodies barely inches apart.

'Not quite everything.'

Jolted by the roughness in his voice, she tried to answer. But before she had a chance even to think about what words to use, let alone form them into a sentence, he took another step closer.

She tried to move, to put some distance between them, but her body was rooted to the floor. The air felt suddenly heavy and tangled, as though the monsoon he'd mentioned earlier was about to break inside the room. Heat was chasing over her cheeks and throat, and then her stomach flipped over as he reached out and, taking her hand, gently slid the wedding ring back on her finger.

'I came to tell you that you do matter. And I do respect you.'

She stared at him. He looked tense, serious, not at all like the teasing, self-possessed man who had dominated her life for the last few days.

'And I do care about your feelings and opinions.'

He paused, and she realised that his hand was still holding hers. It was lucky that he was, for she felt suddenly strangely unsubstantial, as though at any moment she might simply float away.

'Although, given how I've behaved, I can completely see why you would think the opposite.'

Margot stared at him, confused. There was strain in his voice—not anger…uncertainty, maybe—and although he hadn't actually said he was sorry, his words had sounded almost like an apology. Whatever she had expected Max to say, it hadn't been that, and she wasn't sure how to reply.

But the part of her brain that was still functioning prodded her to respond, and so she said the first word that came into her head. 'Okay.'

His eyes bored into hers and she felt her legs wobble, for there was no mockery or hostility in the blue and green of his irises, and no anger in her heart. With a mixture of panic and yearning, she realised that without the restraining presence of their mutual animosity he was too close, that his mouth—that beautiful, temptingly kissable mouth—was dangerously close, and that she was starting to feel dizzy.

Dizzy with…

His hand slid around her waist, and even as her fingers curled into her palms she felt the floor tilt beneath her feet. Every ounce of reason and self-preservation she possessed was telling her to move, to push him away. This—*them*—was a bad idea. She needed to stop it from going any further. Stop it while she still could.

Lifting her hand, she pressed her fists against his chest, meaning to push him away. But somehow her fingers weren't responding. Instead they seemed to be uncurling and sliding over his shoulders, and she couldn't seem to stop herself from gazing at his mouth.

She was giving out all the wrong signals, and yet they felt right—more than right. They felt inevitable and necessary.

'Okay…?' His brows drew together, the muscles in his face tightening with concentration. 'Okay, and now you want me to leave? Or okay, you want me to stay?' he asked hoarsely.

Somewhere inside the wreckage of her brain, it occurred to her that his breathing was as uneven as hers. There was a long, simmering silence. She inhaled shakily. Her body was throbbing with a desperate yearning to feel his soft mouth on hers, to give in to the teasing pleasure of his tongue—only she knew that to tell him that would be foolhardy and self-destructive.

She knew she should lie to him. But she was so sick of lying. Everything else about their relationship might just be for show, but this—this need they felt for each other—was real so why fight it?

'Margot…'

She was suddenly too scared to meet his eyes,

scared that he would see the indecision and the longing in her face.

But, lifting a hand, he cupped her chin and forced her to look at him, and the dark, blazing intensity of his gaze made her breath catch.

'I want you,' he said hoarsely and, lowering his mouth, he brushed his lips momentarily against hers. 'I've wanted you ever since you walked into that boardroom. I want you so badly I can't think straight. I don't even know who I am any more. All I know is that my body burns for you…'

He hesitated, and she could sense that he was steadying himself, that he would stop if she asked him to.

'But you need to tell me what *you* want.'

She stared at him dazedly, her blood humming, an ache of desire spreading out inside her like an oil spill, and then finally she slid her fingers up into his hair and whispered, 'I want you too.'

Lifting her chin with his thumb, he stared down into her eyes for so long that she thought she would fly apart with wanting him, and then slowly he lowered his head and kissed her.

She could hardly breathe. Gently, he parted her lips, pushing his tongue into her open mouth, tasting her, his breath mingling with hers as his fingers slid over the lace of her bodice.

Her skin was growing warm, and an ache that felt both hollow and yet so heavy was spreading out inside her. His fingers were moving ceaselessly, brushing against her breasts, slipping around her waist, and then lower to the curve of her buttocks. She moaned against his mouth and instantly felt his body respond. His fingers grew more urgent, and suddenly he was pulling at the buttons down the back of her dress, and as each button came loose she felt something inside her open up too.

'Max…' she whispered, and her own fingers dropped to the waistband of his trousers and began to tug at the fabric, pressing against the hard outline of his erection.

Max breathed out unsteadily. As his fingers slipped beneath the bodice of her dress he felt his groin harden. Her skin felt impossibly smooth and, lifting his mouth from hers, he buried his lips against her neck, seeking out that pulse at the base of her throat. He felt her stir against him, blindly seeking more, and suddenly he wanted more too. More of that skin, more of her mouth, and more of that pulsing heat that he could feel beneath her dress.

Breaking free, he took a step back and yanked at the collar of his shirt. Ignoring her hands, he tugged it over his head and then, his eyes holding hers, he reached forward and released her shoulders, watching dry-mouthed as the dress slid slowly to the floor.

Underneath she was naked except for a pair of rose-coloured panties tied at the sides with ribbons. Gazing at her naked breasts, he felt his skin catch fire. She was so beautiful—more beautiful than he'd remembered—and, stepping towards her, he tugged her body against his, feeling her nipples harden as they brushed against his bare chest. Lowering his head, he sucked first one and then the other into his mouth, almost blacking out as he felt her squirm beneath his tongue. And then she was pulling at the buckle of his belt, her hands clumsy, her breath suddenly uneven as she freed him from his clothes.

'Margot, Margot—slow down,' he begged. 'Just wait.'

But she wasn't listening, or maybe she was ignoring him. Suddenly he didn't care. Pulling her against him, he lifted her and not quite steadily lowered her onto the bed. Leaning forward, he yanked the ribbons of her panties free, and then she was clutching at his shoulders, pulling him closer, guiding him inside her.

Margot gasped. Looping her arm around his neck, she gripped him tighter, her hips rising, her body opening to meet his thrusts, her hands digging into the muscles of his back. She was shaking with eagerness and relief, for there had never been anyone like him and she knew there never would be. With him, there was no need to think. Everything was pure instinct, and each knew exactly what the other wanted and needed.

As the heat building inside her fanned out like a solar flare she was arching upwards, her thighs splaying, her body gripping him inside and out, until she could hold back no more and she shuddered beneath him. She felt his hands tighten in her hair, his body tense, and then, his breath quickening, he buried his face against her shoulder and, crying out her name, thrust inside her.

CHAPTER SEVEN

IT WAS NEARLY TEN O'CLOCK. Already the quivering sun was high in the sky, and soon the pale sand would be too hot to stand on in bare feet.

Glancing down, Max frowned. As a child, he'd been to the seaside twice—once with his mother and Paul, and once with his school. But it was a long time since he'd walked barefoot anywhere, except between his bathroom and his bedroom or to and from his pool. In fact, it might even be the first time he'd ever been on a beach without shoes as an adult.

But, unusual as that was, walking barefoot couldn't really compete with some of his other more recent and less rational 'firsts'.

Staring out across the bay, to where a couple of seabirds were bobbing peacefully on the water, he ticked them off inside his head.

Obviously getting married to a woman he didn't love or trust took pole position. But a close second was buying those shares from her father.

He'd never paid over the odds for anything and, looking back on it, there had been absolutely no need for him to do so. Although Emile had been maddeningly evasive and capricious, his demand had been modest in comparison to what he'd ended up offering for the shares.

Which brought him to another first—paying for a woman.

Beneath his dark glasses, his eyes narrowed. He didn't like the way it sounded but, despite what he'd said to Margot, and told himself about why he'd married her, that was in essence what he'd done.

And then, of course, last night had been the first time he'd ever chased a woman—or at least followed one.

Watching Margot turn and walk away, he had been too angry to move, his head simmering with barely contained frustration that within the space of a heartbeat she had thrown their honeymoon *and* her ring back in his face. And what had she meant by him not understanding relationships?

He gritted his teeth. He understood relationships perfectly. He should too: he'd had the ultimate learning experience, watching his mother put her life on hold, waiting, hoping—and for what?

For nothing, that was what.

He took a calming breath. No, Margot was wrong. He *did* understand relationships. It was simple, really. If you didn't ask you didn't get.

A wave broke, spilling water over his feet, and he realised that in the time he'd been walking down the beach the tide had begun to turn.

He glanced down at his wrist automatically and frowned. He'd left his watch on the bedside table.

And left Margot sleeping in his bed.

He felt his muscles tighten, heat lapping over his skin like the tide on the beach. In bed, their quarrel had been forgotten, their bodies blurring in a passionate embrace that had shaken him not just physically but emotionally—for he never had felt that close, that committed before. But of course he'd never been married before.

Margot might be sleeping now, but she hadn't slept much last night. Neither of them had. His lips curved upwards. In fact, her curiosity had almost killed them both. But as the dawn had crept into their room he had woken out of habit, and then…

Then he'd had two choices. Stay and wait for Margot to wake too, and carry on where they left off. Or get up and go.

A movement out in the bay caught his eye, and he saw that the two seabirds were squabbling over something—food…territory, maybe.

Whatever it was, their battle was really not that different from his fight with Margot yesterday—every relationship was just a power struggle.

His mouth twisted. But his argument with Margot had been nothing in comparison to the conflict raging inside him when he'd woken this morning.

Stay or leave?

It had been a simple enough choice. Only for some reason he had never struggled so much to make a decision.

His pulse jumped in his throat and he felt an instant answering pulse in his groin. Obviously his body had been urging him to stay. Waking to find her legs tangled between his and her long, silken hair spilling over his chest had felt good—more than good. It had been intoxicating. And as he'd breathed in the scent of her he'd had to force himself back from an edge of almost primal, driving desire.

He stared not quite steadily down the beach, remembering how it had felt to run his urgent hands over her warm skin and feel the sweetness of her tight body gripping his. Watching her beautiful pink lips part and then melt into a half-pout of surrender, he'd lost control. She had been so responsive, so hot.

Even now the memory of the fierce directness of her gaze as he'd moved inside her was turning him inside out. Everything—all the bitterness, the lies, the anger, all of it—had ceased to exist. There had been only Margot, and finally she had been his.

So why had he got up and left?

He drew in a deep breath. He'd thought he had it all figured out. Buy the shares—prove the Duvernays wrong. Marry Margot—prove her wrong. Sleep with Margot—prove her wrong again. Feel better.

His muscles tensed. Only it had been he who had been wrong—times four.

He should have felt sated and complete, and physically he did. Only he hadn't been able to shift a sense that something was missing, or maybe off-key.

He still felt like that now, and that irritated him, for he had no reason to feel that way. Margot was his wife and yesterday, and again and again this morning, she had become his lover, clinging to him, pulling him deep inside her body with a desperation that had matched his own.

Breathing out unsteadily, he wondered why that thought should make his chest tighten?

But it was obvious, really, he thought with relief a moment later.

Even before he'd made his first million, few women—if any—had been out of his reach, and his reputation for playing hard to get was completely justified.

Only ever since he'd walked into the House of Duvernay headquarters his self-control seemed to have gone AWOL.

Yesterday he had been like a starving man, satisfying his hunger. His need to take Margot had been shocking in its urgency, and it had understandably caught him by surprise for he was used to being the one in charge both in business and emotionally. But today, he couldn't pretend that it would be anything other than reckless to show her how much power she had over him.

And that was why he'd had to get up and leave this morning—to demonstrate some of that famed self-control.

So now they were all square. He'd proved his point. Why then was he still here, watching the wildlife and the waves? After all, this was his honeymoon.

Honeymoon—the word and all that it implied ping-ponged inside his head and, feeling his body harden, he turned towards the villa. And then he stopped. Glancing down at the outline of his erection, he breathed out slowly. Perhaps it might be a good idea to wait just a little longer…maybe cool off first. A quick swim would be the perfect way to damp down his libido and dull his senses before seeing Margot again, and it wouldn't hurt to keep her waiting and wanting more.

Without giving himself a chance to change his mind, he tugged his shirt over his head, tossed it onto the sand and began wading purposefully into the water.

Margot woke to sunlight and the sound of waves. It took her perhaps half a second before she realised that she was alone, and that the Max-sized space in the bed beside her was empty.

Rolling over, she touched the pillow. It still had the imprint of his head, and she could smell his aftershave and the scent of his skin, and for some reason she found herself smiling.

It was stupid, really, to feel so happy—probably it was asking for trouble—and yet...

She breathed out slowly.

And yet the strain of the last few days seemed to have lifted from her shoulders. She felt not just spent, but serene, for now she was free to touch Max, and to taste him, to wrap her legs around his quickening body without guilt or shame.

Now that it had happened, she could admit that it had always been just a question of when, not if. But when exactly had it started?

Maybe in the car, when Max had thrown that curveball at her. She had been so angry and hurt.

But then, at the villa, his 'apology'—or at least his honesty following so quickly on the back of their row—had caught her off guard.

Her pulse twitched. Or maybe it had started before that. In the boardroom. Or perhaps when she'd walked past that newsstand in Paris and read his name.

Her name too now!

Max had left his watch on the bedside table and, glancing over at it, she frowned. It was almost midday and she wondered where he was.

Her pulse jitterbugged.

She couldn't remember falling asleep, but she could remember the way he'd curved his hand around her waist, anchoring her to him. Could remember too the way that same hand had cradled her head as his powerful body had thrust into hers.

She had never felt so wanted, so desired—and, okay, it had been just sex, but it had been *real*. Nobody could fake that kind of passion, that kind of tenderness.

And didn't that somehow change things a little between them? Perhaps they could be honest with one another on one level at least.

'You're awake.'

She blinked and, rolling over, she lifted her head and gazed up at him. Max was standing motionless on the deck outside the bedroom, wearing nothing but a pair of faded black shorts, an unbuttoned denim shirt and a pair of dark glasses. Droplets of water clung to the tanned muscular skin of his chest and legs, and his sea-drenched dark hair was moulded to the beautiful bones of his skull.

He looked cool and relaxed and impossibly sexy—like a photo shoot for a modern-day pirate—and as his eyes locked on to hers she felt something tug beneath her skin just as she remembered that she was naked. Her cheeks began to tingle and she felt suddenly shy—which was stupid, really. It wasn't as though he hadn't seen all of her already. And not just seen, she reminded herself, her heart jumping at the memory of how his hands had moved over that same naked skin he was staring at now.

As though reading her mind, he smiled slowly, the edges of his mouth curling up in a way that made her skin instantly grow warmer. Cheeks burning now, she tried to match his smile with a casual one of her own. But it was difficult to act naturally when all she could think about was what else that mouth could and was probably about to do.

Swallowing hard, she sat up and said quickly, 'I didn't hear you get up. I would have come with you.'

His gaze hovered over her flushed face, and

then dropped to the tiny pulse beating at the base of her throat.

'That's okay. You needed to sleep.'

Tugging off his dark glasses, he stepped inside the room and walked slowly across the smooth wooden floor. He stopped beside the bed, and her pulse jumped in her throat as inch by inch his eyes drifted over her bare skin, slowly tracing the contours of her body.

Looking up at him, she felt as if she was floating—and then her heart began beating against her ribcage as, dropping his sunglasses on the bedside table, he leaned forward and kissed her gently on the mouth. She arched her back, her lips parting, and she felt her insides start to melt as he deepened the kiss.

'Sweet...' he murmured against her mouth, and then he was kissing her again, such tender, slow kisses, as though they had the whole of their lives before them.

Which they did, she thought dazedly a moment later, as his hand cupped her breast, his thumb teased the nipple and she felt her body shudder in response.

In an instant he had stolen her thoughts, her identity, even her breath, so that suddenly she was panting. 'Max, please...'

She reached up, blindly seeking more contact, expecting him to move, wanting him to touch her. But he didn't move closer. Instead he ran his hand over her breast and up to her shoulder and then released her.

She stared up at him, her hands balling into fists, her body so hot and tight and tense she thought it would explode.

'I thought—' she began, but her words dried up as he turned and, picking up his watch, frowned down at it.

'Baby, I need a shower and some breakfast. And besides…' His gaze burned into hers and she felt her pulse leap. 'Surely I more than satisfied your curiosity yesterday and this morning.'

Watching him unzip his shorts and push them down over his muscular thighs, Margot felt her stomach flip over. But not from desire this time. His words echoed ominously in her head, and suddenly she knew what he was getting at. It was that stupid, *stupid* remark she'd made in his hotel room, and clearly he'd been waiting for just the right moment to throw it back in her face.

She felt hot and dizzy, anger mingling with shame that she had actually thought Max had wanted her with the same desperate urgency with which she'd wanted him, when all the time it had just been about proving a point.

It might have felt real, but then Max was good at that, she thought savagely—good at making her believe what she wanted to believe. And she'd even given him some help, by listening to that tiny part of her mind that had wanted to be wrong about him, wanted to believe in the fantasy of their explosive sexual chemistry.

A rush of misery and helplessness broke over her, like one of the waves splashing against the shore outside their room. It was the same old story—a story that had started when she was a child, trying to defuse the tension between her parents, and then her father and her grandparents. She was so used to seeking out the good and ignoring the bad that it was almost second nature now for her to spin straw into gold.

Only she wasn't a child any more, and nor was she a spectator. This was her marriage. Her life. And she wasn't just going to stand by with a smile on her face while he played power games.

Her dress—her beautiful wedding dress—lay where Max had pulled it from her frantic body and, sliding out of bed, she picked it up and draped it over one of the cream-coloured armchairs that sat on either side of the doors to the deck.

Stalking into the dressing room, she yanked a pale blue embroidered sundress off the shelf. She pulled it over her head and, without even bothering to look at her reflection or brush her hair, she pushed her feet into some flip-flops and strode onto the deck.

Outside, the beach felt gloriously open and empty. Kicking off her shoes, she walked down to where the lightest imaginable surf was trickling over the sand like champagne foam.

Her mouth thinned. Actually, *not* champagne. She was sick of champagne. Sick of the whole wine-making world and everyone in it. Particularly Max.

She grimaced. Even just thinking about him and his stupid, mammoth ego made her head pound as though she'd drunk a magnum of Grand Cru.

She had thought that having sex with him would be the one true part of their marriage. Only now it seemed that it had been just as superficial and sham as the rest of their relationship—and not just in the present. The memory of what they'd once shared now felt unbearably tainted too.

And she only had herself to blame. She'd known what he was like. Or she should have. After all, what kind of a man blackmailed a woman into marriage?

Her stomach clenched. Sex might have made it feel more intimate and personal, but the truth was that this had never been anything other than a business arrangement—a merger of money and power and status. Anything else was just nonsense, concocted inside her head.

The sound of music and laughter broke into her thoughts and, glancing out to sea, she spotted a cruiser dipping through the water. On the gleaming white deck a group of men and women were dancing, their heads tipped back to the sun, swimsuit-clad bodies radiating heat and happiness.

She stared at them enviously. They seemed so at ease, so uninhibited, and in their loose-limbed freedom they reminded her of Louis and Gisele and their friends. She watched for a moment, lost in her own thoughts, and then, just as she was about to carry on walking, one of the men must have noticed her, for suddenly he was waving, and then they were all waving and calling to her.

It was impossible to hear what they were saying, but their excitement and enthusiasm was infectious, and without even realising that she was doing it she began waving back at them.

'What the hell do you think you're doing?'

A hand gripped her arm and her body was pulled round sharply. Max was standing beside her, wearing a pair of swim-shorts. Her first thought was that he had changed clothes. Her second was that he was incandescent with fury.

She shook his hand off, her own simmering anger rising swiftly to boiling point. 'I would have thought that was obvious. It's called *waving*—'

'Don't give me that.' He interrupted her. 'It's

our honeymoon, and you're standing out here on your own, waving at strangers. What if that had been a boat full of photographers?'

She glared at him. 'It wasn't. And even if it was, what I do or don't do—including waving at strangers on boats—is none of your business. Now, if you're done with throwing your weight around, I'm going to go for a walk.'

Staring down into her defiant face, Max felt his body tense with frustration. It was a feeling that was becoming increasingly familiar since Margot had re-entered his life.

Earlier, returning to the villa from the beach, he had felt the barriers he had so arrogantly created inside his head all but disintegrate as he'd caught sight of her glorious body, spread out so invitingly on the rumpled sheets. Thankfully he had succeeded in hanging on to his self-control by a thread, helped by what must surely have been the coldest shower he'd ever had.

But when he'd walked back into the bedroom his hard-won composure had instantly evaporated as he'd realised that Margot had simply upped and left without so much as a word. His mood hadn't improved as he'd stalked stiffly through the villa. Not wanting to alert his staff to the fact that his wife appeared to have vanished, he'd been forced to pretend that he'd mislaid his phone.

He gritted his teeth. And now, when finally he'd tracked her down, not only was she completely unrepentant, she was clearly looking for a fight.

His eyes narrowed and, by holding his breath, he managed to hang on to his temper. 'Actually I'm far from done. You're my wife now, and if you're expecting our marriage to be civilised—'

'Civilised!' Her gaze clashed with his. 'You don't know the meaning of the word. Do you seriously think it's civilised to just take what you want and move on when you're done—?' She broke off as he started to shake his head.

'So that's what this is about? It was just a shower, Margot.'

The dishonesty of his remark made her breathing jerk in her throat. 'Don't do that, Max. Don't treat me like I'm stupid. It was not *just* a shower. It was you making a point. And I will not let you treat me like some toy you can pick up and play with and then forget about.'

He frowned. 'Are you insane? How could I forget about you? I've just spent the last thirty-five minutes looking for you.'

Her heart was trying to get out of her chest. 'Well, you wasted your time. You might be my husband legally, but our marriage is just a business agreement. It only exists when we're on show, in public—as you just proved to me.'

Max took a step towards her. A thread of fury was soaring up through his body like mercury in a thermometer. He felt breathless with anger and frustration.

'Better that than only existing in the bedroom,' he snarled, unable to hide his emotions any longer.

'What is *that* supposed to mean?' she snapped.

The air around them felt suddenly thick and dark and volatile, like a cloud of bees about to swarm.

'You know exactly what it means. It's the reason you didn't want to marry me all those years ago.'

She glared at him. 'I didn't want to marry you because you only wanted my money. Or have you forgotten telling me that was why you proposed?'

His gaze didn't flicker. 'That was after you'd already let your brother do your dirty work. But the least you could do now is have the guts to tell it like it was.'

'And what was it like, Max?'

His face hardened. 'I was good enough for sex, just not for marriage.'

There was a short, sharp pause. Margot was staring at him as though he'd suddenly started speaking in a foreign language, but he wasn't sure if it was what he'd said or the harshness with which he'd said it that had silenced her.

Margot stared at him in confusion. Her heart was thumping hard against her chest. She was shocked by his words. More shocked still by the fact that he obviously believed them.

Her mouth twisted. Or, more likely, wanted to believe them.

'That's not true—that wasn't how it was! It *wasn't*,' she repeated, as he began shaking his head dismissively.

'Really? Then why were you so worried about keeping us a secret? Oh, sorry, I forgot—' his mouth curled upwards into a sneer '—you were waiting for "the right time" to tell everyone.'

Anger flared inside her. How dared he be so self-righteous? 'Yes, I was. But what was your excuse?' she snapped. 'Because it wasn't just me who wanted to keep our relationship quiet, was it?'

Max breathed out silently. For a moment he thought about telling her the truth. That going public would have meant sharing her with her family, breaking the spell of that summer. And then he came to his senses.

'Nice try. But next to you I'm an amateur when it comes to keeping quiet.'

'What are you talking about?' she said hoarsely.

'I'm talking about when I asked you to marry me before. I gave you a ring. Do you remember what you did? What you said?' His voice was steady, but a muscle was pulsing in his cheek. 'No? Then let me remind you. You did nothing, said nothing. You basically acted like I'd embarrassed you.' His eyes burned into her. 'No, actually, like I'd embarrassed myself.'

She shivered. That wasn't how she remembered it. In her head it had been a moment of shock, drowned out almost immediately by Yves's arrival. Her brother had been white-lipped with rage at what he'd clearly thought was personal betrayal by a man he'd liked and trusted. He'd been angrier, though, with himself, for not protecting her, and so he'd been cruel and unfair. She should have stopped him, only…

'I wasn't embarrassed,' she said slowly. 'I was in shock.'

His mouth thinned. 'Why?' he demanded. 'We'd talked about getting married—'

'Yes, in the *future*.' She stared at him, her pulse stop-starting like a stalled car. 'But not right then. I was nineteen, Max. I was still at university. No, hear me out.' She held up her hands as he started to interrupt. 'You have to understand. I had no idea you were going to ask me. It wasn't in my head. I wasn't ready. I was young and…' She hesitated.

They were heading into dangerous territory, and the thought of confronting what lay ahead made her want to crawl into a darkened room and roll up in a ball. But, looking up at the tense, set expression on his face, she knew that retreating was not an option.

She drew in a breath. 'And I was scared.'

Max stared at her in silence. She was telling the truth. He could hear it in her voice, feel it stinging his skin.

'Why would you be scared?' He'd sounded harsher than he'd intended and she looked over at him. Hearing her breathe out unsteadily, he felt his stomach clench, for he could see that she was still scared now. 'You were scared of *me*?' The thought horrified him so much that he actually couldn't speak any more.

'Of *you*?' She shook her head, eyes widening with horror. 'No, of course not. I was scared of making a mistake, of doing what—'

As she looked up into his eyes he saw her face stiffen, as though she was doing some complicated arithmetic in her head, and then she bit her lip.

'Oh, what's the point? You wouldn't understand.'

For a moment he thought about his own past, and his own private fears. And then he stopped thinking.

Reaching out, he took her hands. 'I might,' he said gently.

He felt her body go rigid, and for a moment he thought she was going to pull away from him, but finally she sighed.

'Okay… This is going to sound crazy, and you probably won't believe me, but when you proposed I wasn't even thinking about us or the ring you'd given me. I was thinking about my mother's engagement ring.'

Hearing the taut note in her voice, Max frowned. It did sound crazy, but for some reason he still believed her.

'I know you probably don't have much interest in celebrity gossip, but you might have heard about my parents?'

He nodded. He could remember his mother following the story in the newspapers, only he'd been too young to care. 'Just the basics. They eloped, and later on your mum accidentally overdosed.' He spoke gently, wanting to ease the impact of his words.

Her face stilled. 'They eloped when she was nineteen. It was a massive scandal. Everyone was looking for them. They ended up hiding in Marrakech, in the house where Louis is staying.'

She smiled bleakly, and he felt something heavy settle on his shoulders at the flash of hurt.

'They were so young and so beautiful, and everyone thought it was incredibly romantic. But it devastated my grandparents, and the reality wasn't romantic at all.'

He felt her fingers tighten around his, and her smile faded.

'They might have looked like the perfect couple from the outside, but honestly, though, their whole relationship started and ended with sex. It wasn't happy or healthy—just compulsive… like an addiction.'

She looked up at him defiantly, only somehow her expression seemed to accentuate her vulnerability.

'And that's what you thought we'd be like?' he asked.

Margot blinked, the directness of his question momentarily silencing her. 'I didn't think anything,' she said finally. 'I just panicked.'

For a moment she considered telling him the *whole* truth. That she'd loved him, and that he was still the only man she'd ever loved. But she'd laid enough of herself bare. Telling the truth now wouldn't alter the facts. Max hadn't loved her then, and he didn't love her now.

Looking back to that devastating moment when his world had imploded, Max felt his chest tighten painfully as for the first time he contemplated a different version of events. And a new and unsettling realisation that he might not only have misjudged Margot all those years ago, but completely overreacted.

'Why didn't you tell me about your parents before?'

She shrugged, and the resignation in that simple gesture made his breath catch in his throat.

Looking down at her feet, she began digging her bare toes into the sand. 'I suppose I didn't know if I could trust you.'

He frowned. 'Is that why you kept us a secret?'

She didn't answer for a moment, and then slowly she shook her head. 'Maybe at first. But not later. Then I wanted it to be just you and me. I love my family, but they can be so demanding.'

'You mean your father?'

Margot stared at him. For a moment she'd actually forgotten that Max had met Emile. She gave him a weak smile. 'I hear you woke him up.'

Max grimaced. 'I paid for those shares in ways you'll never know.'

He was attempting a joke, trying to lighten the mood, but she couldn't shift the memory of his accusation.

She bit her lip. 'You were wrong, Max. I was never ashamed of you. I just knew that if I told my family they would complicate things. It's what they do.'

He stared down at her, his eyes glittering strangely. 'And what do *you* do?'

'Me? I'm a fixer-upper.'

That was an understatement. She seemed to have spent most of life problem-solving for her family, and with a tiny wrench of doubt she wondered what would happen if she just stopped. Was that why they loved her? For what she could do for them, not who she was.

Swallowing the lump of misery in her throat, and fearing she had given too much away, she shrugged. 'I make it all look perfect—which with my family is practically a full-time job. They might look flawless from the outside, but my father is living proof that appearances can be deceptive.'

Max hesitated. For a moment he stared at her in silence, as though working something out in his head, and then, taking a step closer, he pulled her into his arms.

'True,' he said slowly. 'But sometimes things are what they appear to be. Like the chemistry between us. That's real. You can't fake it, or pretend it doesn't exist.' Gently he reached up and stroked her hair. 'You were right about this morning. I was trying to prove a point. Only unfortunately I've just ended up proving what an idiot I am.'

He stared down at her, trying to make sense

of everything that was going on inside his head. Coming down to the beach, his anger had been hot and righteous, but now her honesty, and the courage it had taken for her to be so honest, made him feel angry with himself. Margot was not the person he had thought she was. She was not selfish or self-absorbed. On the contrary, she seemed to have spent most of her life sacrificing herself to the demands of her family.

Breathing out softly, he slid his hand under her chin and tilted her face upwards. 'Why do you think I changed my mind about going back to France?'

Margot stared at his face in silence, not understanding why he was asking her that question now, and wondering where the conversation was heading.

His grip tightened. 'Because I want you as much as you want me, Margot. More than I've ever wanted any woman. I didn't want a honeymoon just because of what people might say if we didn't have one.' He smiled faintly. 'I think you know me well enough to believe that I can hold my own in the world.'

She nodded mutely, her heart hammering in her chest as his smile twisted.

'But clearly I haven't given you reason enough to believe that changing my mind was not an act of complete thoughtlessness. So let me make it clear now. Changing our plans wasn't supposed to upset you or your family. But I know now that it did, and I'm sorry. For not talking to you about it first. And for being a jerk this morning.'

Lifting her hand to his mouth, he kissed it lightly.

'I know I haven't covered myself in glory these last few days, but I'm not a monster.' He stared down into her eyes. 'It's not too late to fly back. If that's what you want, then tell me and I'll make it happen.'

Margot bit her lip. It was an olive branch, or maybe an attempt at reparation...

'You'd do that? For me?'

His fingers closed more firmly around hers. 'Of course. You're my wife. I'm not in the habit of making empty promises. I made vows, and I meant them.'

She wondered what he meant by empty promises, but something in his expression warned her that now was not the time to ask him.

It's not too late to fly back. I made vows, and I meant them.

Gazing up at him, his words echoing inside her head, Margot was torn. Part of her wanted to make things right with her grandfather. But Max had apologised, and he'd admitted that he wanted her. That the attraction between them was special. For a moment she was in a daze, but as she caught sight of her wedding ring she made up her mind.

'I want to stay. But I'd like us to talk to my grandfather and Louis.'

His expression didn't change, but he wrapped his arms around her, pulled her closer, and she felt his heart beating unsteadily.

'Then that's what I want too,' he said softly.

CHAPTER EIGHT

ROLLING ONTO HER FRONT, Margot closed her eyes and let the book she'd been failing to read slip from her fingers.

After a night in Max's arms she was feeling drowsy and sybaritic, so she had decided to spend an hour by the pool. The sun felt wonderful on her bare skin, and she was feeling wonderful too, the tranquillity of her mind complementing the languor of her body.

It wasn't just the heat that was making her feel so relaxed. Today felt almost like a new beginning, for finally she had told her family about her marriage.

She had spoken first to her grandfather and then to Louis, and even now she couldn't quite believe how well it had gone. It had been so much easier than she'd expected—mainly thanks to Max.

He had been with her the whole time, literally holding her hand. Remembering his quiet but easy self-assurance, she felt her pulse jump. She doubted there were many people who had the charisma and confidence to manage a man of her grandfather's status and gravitas. But, hearing Max talk, she had known that nobody would question the validity of their marriage. He had seemed utterly unfazed, and his certainty had been irresistible.

But then everything about Max was irresistible. His looks, his resoluteness and his power were an aphrodisiac that made her ache to feel his hands on her body again.

Pushing aside an image of what those hands could do, she wondered how and when he'd learned to behave with such poise. He might be her husband, but his background was still as much of a mystery to her as it had been nearly ten years ago.

Stretching her arms out, she shifted against the cushion of the sun lounger and thought back to their argument on the beach, and the confession that had spilled out of her afterwards. Their anger had been so intense it had felt like a storm cloud breaking. Only somehow, out of her fury and his, they had come to a better understanding.

Her skin began to prickle. Or rather *he* now understood *her*, for the sharing of information had been entirely on her side.

She hadn't meant to confide in him about her

parents' relationship, but between the endless blue of the ocean and the relentless blue and green of his gaze there had been nowhere to hide.

And, even though she had never put it into words before, it had been easy to tell him the truth—maybe because he had listened to her in a way that no one else had ever done. Her staff hung on her every word at work, and her family were always asking for advice, but Max had really *listened* to her, as if she mattered to him. And it had been his concentration and persistence which had finally broken down the barriers she'd built to stop the prying gaze of the world.

Remembering his remark about empty promises, she wondered what he'd meant. She would have liked to ask him, only his manner had not exactly encouraged further discussion. And it had been no different in the past. If ever she had tried to ask him about himself he had simply batted her questions away and changed the subject.

Aged nineteen, she'd thought it didn't matter that she hardly knew anything about him. In truth, she'd been too in love, and too astonished that he was no longer treating her just as Yves's younger sister but as a woman, to do anything but bask in his attention.

There had been other reasons, too, why she

had purposely not cross-examined him. As someone who valued her own privacy, she was sympathetic to other people's reticence, and so she'd been if not happy then understanding of his silence.

But now…?

She sighed. They might have reached a kind of truce, but no matter how much she would have liked to peek into the complexities of Max's mind she wasn't feeling nearly brave enough to question him about his background or his private life.

Or, worse, his feelings.

And maybe she didn't need to, for when her body was pressed against his, and she could feel his heart beating in time to hers, she felt as if she knew everything there was to know about him.

She felt a pang of remorse as she remembered how she'd accused him of being insensitive and self-serving.

He wasn't. She knew that now. He was capable of compassion and, unlike a lot of people with money and power, capable and willing to apologise.

Realising how much he had upset her, he had offered to return to France, and even though she had agreed to stay at the villa she knew that he had meant what he'd said. And, athough she had wanted to tell her family in person, she didn't regret her decision. On the contrary, right now she could think of nowhere she'd rather be—so much so that she was struggling to remember why she had ever thought that having a honeymoon was such a bad idea.

She felt a warm, tingling feeling in the pit of her stomach. After they'd called her grandfather Max had led her back to the bedroom and stripped both of them naked, his mouth urgently seeking hers, kissing her so deeply that she was breathless and dizzy. And, curling her legs around him, her hands shaking with eagerness as they'd spread over the muscles of his back, she had guided him inside her restless, aching body.

Lifting her head, she turned her face away from the sun. But it wasn't just about the sex. Max was great company too. He was well-read, and interested in what she'd read—they had talked about everything from tax reform to the rise in popularity of Peruvian food. And he made her laugh—*really* laugh—in a way she had almost forgotten she could.

It was easy to see why her teenage self had fallen under his spell. And here in the sunshine, far away from the relentless, unforgiving demands of real life, it would be as easy to feel the same way about him now.

Her stomach clenched. Easy, but terrifying at the same time.

For despite knowing that she was letting herself get swept away by the romantic setting and the new openness between them, the truth was that a part of her had always wanted to believe in him—to reimagine their history with a happy ending.

And, even though it was stupid and pointless and crazy, even dangerous to think that way, with every hour that passed she just couldn't seem to stop herself wanting to believe that their intimacy and mutual hunger for one another was more than just physical attraction.

A pair of warm hands slid over her back and her pulse darted forward like a startled fish.

'Hey, sleepyhead.'

Max nuzzled her neck, and she felt heat rush to the spot where his lips were caressing her bare skin. Tipping her head back slightly, she let her cheek graze his, breathing in the mix of coffee and cologne and some undefined but potent essence of maleness that made her heat rush through her body.

Rolling over onto her back, she opened her eyes and gazed up at him, wondering if she would ever get used to how gorgeous he was. Stomach flipping, she reached out and curled her hands around his biceps, her thumbs pressing into the hard muscles.

'I'm not sleeping, I'm worshipping the sun,' she protested, a beat of blood starting to drum inside her head. 'Why don't you join me?'

Gently cupping her face in his hand, he lowered his mouth, brushing his lips against hers. 'I'd much rather worship you,' he whispered.

He raised his head, and the intent in his beautiful eyes made her body feel suddenly boneless.

'But, as I'm very devout, and it may take me some time, I think we should go somewhere a little more comfortable,' he said softly. And, pulling her to her feet, he led her back to their bedroom.

They made slow, passionate love all morning, stopping only for Max to crawl out of bed and bring back some lunch, which they ate with their fingers.

Later, they walked along the shoreline, happy just to hold hands and pick up shells and pieces of driftwood, until finally it became too hot and they retreated to the villa and to bed again.

'Are you okay?'

Margot glanced up at Max. She was lying in his arms, her body damp and feverish, still trying to catch her breath. 'I am—are you?'

His eyes were dark and lazy as they rested on her face.

'Yes, but…' He paused, his hand caressing the curve of her hip in a way that made her body start to shake inside.

'But what?' she asked quickly, knowing that if she waited too long to reply her skin would grow warm and she would rapidly lose the power of both thought and speech.

He sounded casual, but in contrast his expression was tense, expectant. 'I need to make a phone call.'

What? Now? Can't someone else do it?

Her disappointment was instant, and clearly it must have showed on her face for, grimacing, he shook his head and answered her unspoken questions. 'I can't delegate this one, but it won't take long.' His gleaming eyes drifted hungrily over her naked body. 'I promise.'

Kissing her lightly on the lips, he slid out of bed and tugged on a pair of linen trousers.

Staring at him, she frowned. 'Where are you going?'

'I'm going to use the study. I have to,' he said as she started to protest. 'There's no way I can concentrate with you here like—'

His words faltered as she leaned back against the pillow and moistened her lips. 'Like what?' she asked innocently.

He groaned. 'Margot, please don't make this any harder than it already is,' he said hoarsely.

Tilting her head to one side, she smiled. 'Make *what* harder, Max?'

'Very funny.'

His eyes narrowed, and the slow, hot glance he gave her made her heart ping-pong inside her chest. 'Do not leave this bed. I'll be ten minutes, tops, and then you and I are going to…'

She held his gaze, and there was a moment of pure, pulsing silence.

And then, his jaw tightening, he swore forcefully. 'Ten minutes,' he said softly, and before she had a chance to reply he turned and walked swiftly out of the room.

Watching him leave, Margot rolled over and pulled his pillow against her stomach, wanting to capture the last traces of warmth from his body.

It was silly, really, given that it was only lust, but the fact that he clearly wanted her so badly made her feel ludicrously happy, even though the space in the room where he'd been made her feel empty inside.

It was annoying that work had intruded, but in a way she was pleased that he was so committed to making good on his promise to turn her business around. He'd made at least one call a day since they'd arrived at the villa, usually while she was in the pool or taking a shower.

But they were always short, and afterwards he was doubly attentive.

Clutching the pillow tighter, she wrapped the still-warm sheet around her naked body and, listening to the calming rhythm of the sea, imagined his return…

She must have dozed off. Waking, and aware of a shift in the light, she reached over to the bedside table and picked up her phone. Glancing at the screen, she frowned. Max had said ten minutes, but he'd been gone more like twenty-five.

She bit her lip, uncertain of whether to stay in bed or go and find him. Reluctant to move, she fell back against the pillow. He would probably be back soon, she told herself.

But after another five minutes she couldn't bear it any longer. Sliding out of bed, she picked up the shirt that he'd discarded the night before and pulled it over her head.

As usual, aside from the sound of the surf, the villa was still and quiet. The staff were not just discreet, they were virtually invisible—since that first day, she had only seen Aurelie, the housekeeper, once.

In the hallway, she headed towards the study, but as she reached the half-open door she hesitated as she heard Max's voice. If he'd been talking to a member of his staff then she would have walked right in, and had he sounded angry she would probably have sneaked away. But he wasn't angry, and he definitely wasn't talking to his PA or his accountants or his lawyer.

Her pulse stumbled.

She couldn't hear exactly what he was saying, but there was a warmth and ease to his voice—a tenderness that made her hands start to shake. It was the kind of shared tenderness that only two people in a long and close relationship would have, and she knew instinctively that he was talking to a woman.

And not just any woman—a woman he loved very much.

For a moment she couldn't move. Her legs seemed to have turned to ice. And then, breathing out unsteadily, she took hold of the handle and slowly pushed the door open.

Max had his back to her. He was gazing out of the window, his phone pressed against the side of his head, and suddenly the blood was roaring in her ears—for this was almost exactly how she'd found him in the boardroom. Only then he'd been sitting down, wearing a suit, and now he was standing bare-chested, shifting restlessly, the hard, primed muscles of his beautiful athlete's body rippling as he talked.

'Look, I have to go now.'

The gentleness in his voice made her feel hollowed out with misery.

'I know. I wish you were here with me too. But I'll speak to you tomorrow, I promise.'

He rang off, and she watched his fingers curl around the phone, her pulse staggering, her chest so tight she thought it would burst. And then he turned and saw her. And, however bad she had felt moments before, she knew that nothing in her life would ever hurt as much as seeing his face and the truth in his eyes.

'How long?' she whispered. Her throat was so constricted that it hurt to speak, but the pain was nothing to the pain in her chest. 'How long?' she repeated, more loudly this time. 'How long have you been seeing her?'

He stared at her blank-eyed. 'I think you must be a little confused—' he began.

But she cut across him, for there was no way she could listen to any more of his lies.

'No, actually, I think I was a *lot* confused. So confused, in fact, that I'd actually started to believe that you wanted to make this work.' Her mouth curved with contempt. 'What was it you said? *"I'm not in the habit of making empty promises."*' Clenching her teeth, fighting the desolation and despair clogging her throat, she shook her head. 'I'm such an idiot. I really thought you were talking about me, when all the time you were talking about your mistress!'

'Mistress!'

His face hardened, and before she had a chance to register the flash of white-hot anger in his eyes he had crossed the room in three strides.

'You clearly are confused if you think I'd ever make any woman my mistress.'

'Don't lie to me, Max,' she exploded, his denial lighting the fuse of her shock and anger. 'I heard you. I heard you talking to her—'

'No, you didn't, Margot.' His mouth twisted, and she could see the muscles in his arms and chest straining. 'You heard me talking to my mother.'

There was a dull, heavy silence. She stared at him, almost floating with shock, her anger swept aside by his words. Up until that moment she'd never heard him refer to any kind of relative, even in passing. In fact, she'd thought that maybe he didn't actually have any family, and that was why it had been easy for him to be so blasé and dismissive about hers.

'Your mother?'

'Yes. My mother.'

There was a different tone to his voice now—a roughness that wrenched at something inside her, made her want to reach out to him. As if he sensed that, he turned abruptly and walked towards the window.

Staring after him, Margot swallowed. His back was towards her, and she could see the effort with which he was holding himself still, holding in the emotion which had split his voice.

'Max—' She took a step forward and then stopped, her pulse skipping a beat. She knew his anger—knew that it could be ice-cold or like a fire beneath his skin. But this was different. If it was anger, then it was a desperate and stricken kind that she had never seen before.

His shoulders tensed, and his breathing was ragged. 'Just go, Margot.'

He couldn't bear to look at her, to have to see what she was feeling.

'No. I'm not going anywhere.'

She spoke softly, as if she was unsure as to how or even if he would respond, but even without seeing her face he could sense that she meant what she was saying.

Turning slowly, he stared at her in silence.

Mistress.

How could one word cause so much pain? But was it that surprising, given that it embodied both his mother's crushed hopes and his own sense of helplessness? A helplessness he couldn't let Margot see.

Only there was no way out, for she was standing just inside the room, her body blocking the doorway.

'This is not your problem,' he said flatly.

Shaking her head, she took a step closer. 'Yes, it is. You see, I made promises too.'

'Yes—under duress.'

He had made her do it so that he could right an alleged wrong. Or that was what he'd told himself. But marrying Margot had never really been about getting his money's worth for her father's shares, or punishing her for not wanting him ten years ago. The truth was both simple and more complex. Only he'd never discussed his mother with anyone—never so much as hinted at the turmoil of his past—and he didn't know what to say or even how to start now.

Brown eyes flaring, she held his gaze. 'That's not true. I had choices, and I walked into that chapel willingly.'

She hesitated, and before he had a chance to react she had taken two quick steps forward and taken his hand.

'And I'm here willingly too.' She hesitated again. 'Are you okay?'

He could hear that she was worried about him, see by the slight tremble of her mouth that she cared, and that in itself made his head spin. But it was her touch, gentle but firm, that convinced him to tell her the truth. For she was standing in front of him not as some bargaining chip or sacrifice but as an equal. And as for telling a difficult truth—hadn't she done that herself, yesterday?

He nodded. 'She worries about me if I don't ring when I say I'm going to ring. That's why I couldn't stay with you earlier.'

Margot nodded. He was keeping his promises. Her head was filled with a blur of questions and conjecture but, glancing up at him, she knew there was only one question she needed to ask right now.

'Is everything all right?'

His face tightened. 'She misses me. But I've talked to her and she's okay now.'

Margot nodded. More than anything she wanted to stay on the island with Max but, remembering his reaction when she'd got upset about her grandfather, she didn't hesitate. 'Do you need to go back?'

He shook his head slowly. 'She has people with her. They're good—not just professional, but kind. She trusts them.'

A pulse was throbbing in the side of her head. 'Is your dad not around?'

She gazed at him uncertainly. Even as she had spoken she'd wondered why she didn't already know the answer to such a basic question. And why it felt as if his answer would be the key to unlocking this complex, compelling man who had dominated her life since she was a teenager.

Slowly he shook his head again. 'He's never been around. The relationship was over before she even found out she was pregnant. She told him, but—' Catching sight of her face, he shrugged. 'It's fine. You can't miss what you don't know.'

Thinking about her own childhood, and how much she'd longed for her life to be simple and stable, Margot wasn't sure if she agreed with him. But she was too scared to say so for fear of disturbing the thread of his thoughts and derailing this uncharacteristic openness on his part.

'I suppose not. But it must have been hard for her by herself.'

She felt his fingers tense, and then tighten around hers.

'She managed okay.' His eyes were intent on her face. 'And she wasn't always by herself. When I was about eleven she met this guy called Paul. She was working as a receptionist at a law firm, and he was one of the clients.'

'What was he like?'

He turned towards her, the hazy sunlight floating into the room making his eyes glitter like gemstones.

'I was eleven. I don't think I knew what he was like.' He gave her a crooked smile. 'He ran a logistics company. But as far as I was concerned he had three cars—two of them convertibles—and he supported the same football team as me, so I thought he was cool.'

His face softened.

'And he made my mum happy. She always used to worry so much about money, and work, and me, but after she met Paul she seemed to relax. I guess it was good for her to have someone around she could rely on.'

Margot nodded. She knew exactly how Max's mother must have felt. The relief of not being alone, of not always having to be the person in charge.

'We moved into a new house, and Paul more or less moved in with us. He was away on business a lot, but it didn't matter. By then I'd worked out that he wasn't that interested in me. But that didn't matter either, because he took us on holiday and he bought me new football boots.'

He paused.

'Only it was different for my mum. I knew she really wanted to marry him. I asked him about it once, but he said it was too soon and that he needed to get his business established. He gave her a necklace instead of a ring, and then I went to boarding school and I suppose I just forgot about it.'

Something in his voice pulled her chest tight,

but she made herself say lightly, 'Did you like school?'

He shrugged. 'It was fine. I was good at most things, and I was in the football and rugby squads, so I was always training or playing matches. I didn't really have time to get home-sick.'

She felt it again—this time in her throat. A tightening, almost a nervousness, and then her heart began to beat a little faster. 'But you did go home?'

His shoulders were so rigid now it looked as though they would snap. 'Only Saturday after-noons, after the match. Except this one time.'

The muscles in his arms shifted and tensed.

'Why? What happened?' Holding her breath, she waited for him to answer.

'I'd been away at school about a year. It was the end of November and the school boiler broke. We got sent home, only some of us decided not to go home. We went into Paris instead. And that's when I saw him.'

She saw that Max was staring out of the win-dow, except a moment later she realised he was actually staring at their reflection.

'We were walking past a restaurant and he was inside, sitting at a table with this woman and three children—a boy and two girls. And that's when I realised. It wasn't that he didn't want to marry my mum. He couldn't. Because he was already married.'

Margot felt her stomach coil in on itself.

'That's awful. Did you tell her?'

For a moment he didn't reply, and the silence seemed to stretch out of the room and across the ocean to the blurred line of the horizon.

'I didn't have to,' he said finally. 'She already knew. She'd known for years and she'd just been waiting and hoping.' He shook his head. 'I got mad—*really* mad with her. I told her she had to have it out with Paul and give him an ultimatum.' He smiled tightly. 'You know how I love an ultimatum.'

He was attempting to make a joke, but the weariness in his voice made the breath catch in her throat.

'And then what happened?'

'She confronted him. And he told her that even if he hadn't already been married, she wasn't "wife material". That women like her were only good for sex.'

She groped for something to say but she couldn't speak. In part she was stunned by the brutality of Paul's remarks, but what had left her speechless was the fragment of memory rising to the surface of her thoughts. Max's accusation on the beach that he had been *"good enough for sex, just not for marriage"*.

At the time she'd thought he was just throwing out insults. Now, though, she saw that his choice of words had been deliberate. And now she knew why. Ten years ago, when she had been too stunned to speak in his defence, he had thought—understandably—that history was repeating itself, that she was judging him as Paul had judged his mother.

Her heart contracted and she felt a sudden overwhelming urge to cry—for she could see now that her silence had been as cruel as Paul's words. Not only had she hurt him, she had reinforced his deep-rooted fear that he wasn't good enough. No wonder he had wanted her father's shares so badly. He had wanted to prove himself—prove her wrong.

Max breathed out unsteadily. He had never talked so much, or so openly. He felt drained but, looking at Margot's face, he could see only concern, and that gave him the strength to continue.

'I don't think he liked being made to feel like the bad guy, so that was it. He broke up with her. Stopped paying the rent and my school fees. My mum had a kind of breakdown. She couldn't leave the house, let alone work. She still can't. That's why she didn't come to the wedding. She couldn't have—not even if it had been in France.' He threw her a small, stiff smile. 'In the end, we got this apartment in Saint-Denis. You might have heard of it?'

She nodded and, looking past her, he gritted his teeth. Of course she'd heard of it. The tenth *arrondissement* was notorious for its sprawling concrete estates and for having a higher than average crime rate.

Even now he could still remember moving into the apartment, with its broken windows and graffiti-covered door. In no time at all his mother had retreated into herself, and he had begun truanting and dabbling in petty crime.

He gave a humourless laugh. 'It was a difficult time. Moving house, changing school, and then my mum being so crushed. I started getting into trouble at school—if I even went. Smoking, stealing, fighting... And then I surpassed myself and broke into Paul's office.'

Watching her face, he gave a sardonic smile.

'Don't worry! You're not married to a criminal. Weirdly, Paul came down and talked to the police and they let me off. And then he got me a job, helping out at his friend's vineyard. The first day I helped graft a vine and I was hooked. Five years later I ended up working for Yves, and the rest you know.'

He stopped abruptly. After the closeness of his confession the sudden silence was such a shock that all she wanted to do was to fill the void, so she said the first thing that came into her head. 'Why do you think Paul helped you?'

He frowned. 'I think he felt guilty about what he'd said to my mother, and how he'd treated her, and maybe even me too.'

Eyes narrowing, she nodded slowly. 'So he should.'

The indignation in her voice made him smile properly. 'And there I was, thinking you'd be all for putting me in handcuffs.'

Their gazes locked and a pulse of heat began to beat over her skin. 'Thinking or hoping?' she asked softly.

He breathed in sharply and she reached out for him and suddenly he was pulling her closer and burying his face into her hair. 'I'm sorry,' he murmured.

'For what? I was the one making stupid assumptions and even stupider accusations. And if you're talking about our marriage,' she added fiercely, 'then I meant what I said earlier. I walked into that chapel willingly. And I'd walk into it again now.'

As she spoke her heart gave a jolt, and she felt something inside her splitting apart and, with a mixture of fear and relief, she realised that for her their relationship was way more than physical. That at some unspecified point she had opened her heart to him.

For a moment she came dizzyingly close to telling him that she still loved him—more so even than she had before. And not just willingly, but unconditionally. But, glancing up at his set face, she knew that this was not about her and her feelings.

He stared down at her, his face still strained. 'That doesn't mean I'm not sorry for putting you in an impossible situation.' He hesitated. 'And that isn't the only reason I'm sorry.' Lifting his head, he looked down at her. 'When I met you, I was still a mess.'

She gave him a small, swift smile. 'You looked pretty good to me.'

His mouth curled upwards. 'On the outside, maybe. But everything had been so difficult for so long. When we got together I didn't want to be like my mum—just sitting around, waiting and wishing. I wanted to be in control.'

He frowned. It was the first time he'd ever articulated those thoughts to himself, let alone out loud, but for some reason—maybe the firmness of her arms around his waist, or the softness in her eyes—he wanted her to know them.

'Deep down, I think I knew it was too soon, and that you weren't ready, but I just wanted things to be definite between us—that's why I proposed. Only then Yves turned up, and he was so appalled and so opposed to even the idea of it—'

'He was shocked,' Margot said quickly. 'He felt the same way I did about our parents' marriage. I promise you, it would have been the same with any man.'

He frowned. 'I want to believe you, and maybe I can now. But he made me feel stupid and small, and you didn't say anything. I was angry and upset. So I told you that I'd only wanted you for your money. But I didn't. It was a lie. I just wanted to hurt you.'

Margot stared at him, misery swelling in her chest, seeing that moment as though from his perspective. Of course he'd been hurt. Yves had been brutal, and in her silence she had only condoned his brutality.

It was all such a mess.

They had both assumed the worst of each other. But by trying not to repeat the mistakes of the past they had succeeded in ruining their future together.

She bit her lip. 'I should have stopped Yves. If I'd said something—'

He looked down at her hand in his, and for a moment she thought he was going to release his grip. But instead he lifted her fingers, tilting her rings up to the light.

'It wouldn't have made any difference. He was

too angry and upset. We all were. And it doesn't matter any more, anyway. It might have taken us a long time to get here, but everything's worked out fine.'

His eyes on hers were soft, and she felt warmth spread over her skin.

'You're my wife, and we're together now. That's all that matters.'

She was breathless from his nearness. It was all she could do to stay standing as he cupped her face in his hands and kissed her. Her heart wanted to burst, for she couldn't ignore the facts. She might want Max to love her but he didn't. Not then and not now.

But as his fingers slid under her shirt all conscious thought was swept away. One hand splayed out over the skin of her back, the other tugged at her buttons until her shirt fell open and she felt cool air wash over her stomach and breasts. Her nipples tightened and, moaning softly, she reached out and touched his chest.

Breathing in sharply, he pulled her against him...

CHAPTER NINE

HER HEART WAS beating hard and fast. Her hands slid up through his dark hair and she moved backwards clumsily, his arm guiding her. Or was she pulling him? And then he was lifting her onto the desk, sweeping papers aside and lowering her to the gleaming wood.

For a moment he watched her, his eyes dark and glittering with desire, and then, breathing shallowly, he leaned over and kissed his way down her neck to her breast, rolling his tongue around first one rosy-tipped nipple then the other.

Arching upwards, she gasped, and then she collapsed back against the desk as he dropped to his knees and took her with his mouth.

Panting, she shifted against him, raising her hips, her body already starting to tremble, wanting more. And then her fingers tightened in his hair and she pulled him up. Her hands fumbled with the button on his trousers and suddenly she was pulling him free, her fingers closing around him in a fist.

He grunted, catching her hand with his. He pushed it away and, raising her up, thrust inside her, flattening her body with his.

'Look at me,' he muttered.

Wrapping her legs around his hips, she gazed up at him as he pushed harder and deeper, the blaze in his eyes matching the burning heat between her thighs. Suddenly she was grasping his head in her hands, her muscles clenching as he surged into her again and again, and then, tensing, she cried out, her body joining his in a shuddering climax.

Feeling him bury his face in her throat, Margot closed her eyes and breathed out shakily. She couldn't move, certainly couldn't speak. And she didn't want to. All she wanted to do was lie there in his arms for ever, breathing in the air that he breathed.

She felt him shift above her and, feeling his gaze, she opened her eyes. He was gazing down at her, his face flushed, his breathing unsteady.

'Are you okay? I didn't hurt you, did I?'

She shook her head. 'This desk is actually more comfortable than it looks.'

Lifting her hand, she traced her finger along his jawline and over the shadow of stubble on his chin.

Frowning, he gently withdrew and pulled her upright, supporting her with his arm. 'I kept thinking we should go the bedroom, but I was desperate.'

She smiled. 'I don't know whether to be offended that you were clear-headed enough to think anything at all, or flattered that you were so desperate.'

Stroking her blonde hair away from her face, his gaze held hers. He smiled. '"Clear-headed" might be pushing it.' He kissed her lightly on the lips then, dipping his mouth to her throat, brushed the sensitive skin of her collarbone and the slope of her breast. 'I don't know what happens when I'm with you but it's got very little to do with thinking. Just wanting. And feeling.'

Her heart gave a lurch, but she knew that the feelings he was talking about were physical, not emotional, and sexual desire was nothing like love.

Blocking the ache in her chest, and keeping the smile on her face, she said lightly, 'Me too.'

Breathing out, Max pulled her closer. Tipping her head back, he kissed her deeply, and as her nipples brushed against his chest he felt her stir restlessly against him. Instantly his body began to throb in response.

Moaning softly, she broke the kiss, and pressed a hand to the middle of his chest. 'Max…'

'Yes, Margot?' he said hoarsely.

'Do you think we could make it to the bed-room this time?'

He nodded slowly, his eyes on her mouth, and then, grabbing her wrist, he tugged her towards the door.

Later they swam in the pool and lay in the sun.

'Is this okay for you?' Margot glanced over at him, frowning slightly. *She* didn't actually want to go anywhere or do anything, but then she was in love. All she wanted to do was spend every minute of every hour with Max, savouring every moment, absorbing every detail.

But she wasn't ready to reveal her true feelings to him yet—in fact she wasn't sure that she would ever be ready. It had been hard enough to explore her own. Having to face up to the fact that Max couldn't and wouldn't ever share those feelings was not worth spoiling this new intimacy between them for. And besides, right now his body inside and beneath and on top of hers was enough.

She cleared her throat. 'I mean, we haven't ac-tually left the villa once, and we've only got an-other five days. Is there nothing you'd rather do?'

His eyes rested intently on hers, and she shook her head, her mouth curving into a smile.

'You have a one-track mind.'

'It's not one-track,' he said lazily, reaching over to caress her hipbone in a way that made heat rush though her. 'It's just one destination.'

She reached for his hand, intending to still it, knowing that if she didn't she'd be begging him to take off her clothes—take *her*, full stop, out on the terrace. But his fingers curled around her wrist and he pulled her towards him, so that her stomach was pressing against the hot, toned muscles of his abdomen.

For a moment she stared at him, dry-mouthed. She loved what they shared, loved the press of his mouth on hers, the touch of hand and the weight of his body. Only, feeling as she did, she knew she should be careful. Wrapped in his arms, it was temptingly, dangerously easy for her to start fantasising about true love and happy endings, for that was when they were at their most intimate. But every time she thought about taking a step back she only had to look at him and she was struggling to breathe.

The trouble was that her hunger for him far outweighed her willpower, and each time she gave in to that hunger it got harder and harder not to tell him how she felt.

'What is it?'

He was staring at her, studying her closely so that for one terrible moment she thought she must somehow have revealed her thoughts.

'Nothing.' She gave him a casual smile. 'It just seems a shame to come all this way and not even have a look around. It's so beautiful… I'm sure there must be something stunning to see.'

His eyes slid slowly over the three turquoise triangles tied around her body. 'That bikini is pretty stunning.'

She rolled her eyes. 'I was talking about sight-seeing.'

He grinned. 'In that case, now you come to mention it, there is something I'd like to take a closer look at. You have this tiny little scar, just below your—'

Reaching over, she punched him lightly on the arm and he broke off, laughing.

'You're impossible!' She was laughing too. 'People do other things on their honeymoon beside tearing each other's clothes off.'

'And is that what you want to do? Other things? Like sightseeing.'

Assuming that he was still teasing her, and about to respond in kind, she looked up, her mouth curving at the corners. But as their eyes met she felt her heart start to pound. Max was smiling, but his eyes were serious, expectant, as though her answer mattered. Her smile seemed suddenly out of place. Why was he asking? Did he think that she was bored? Or that she wanted to be somewhere else, *with* someone else?

Meeting his gaze, she shook her head. 'No, I'm happy being here with you, relaxing,' she said carefully. 'I just wasn't sure if that was what *you* wanted.'

'I don't care what we do as long as I'm with you.' Leaning forward, he tipped her face upwards and kissed her softly on the mouth. 'That's all I want—to be with you.'

Letting her lashes shield her eyes, she kissed him back, feeling a shot of pure, sweet happiness. Maybe it was cowardly not to tell him the truth, but kisses were so much simpler than feelings—and even more so when his feelings were so far removed from hers.

Lying back on the lounger, Max stretched out his legs, closing his eyes to the beat of the sun. Despite his easy words he felt a ripple of unease snake across his skin, only he wasn't entirely sure why.

These last few days had been hard. Arguing with Margot, seeing her so upset and then confessing his past to her had been painful. But it had been worth it, for now he had everything he'd ever wanted. He was the biggest shareholder in one of the oldest and most prestigious champagne businesses in the world and, more importantly, Margot was his wife.

His life was complete, and he should be enjoying that fact. He *wanted* to enjoy it, but he wasn't. Instead he felt restless and uneasy.

Watching Margot turn the pages of her book, a tiny frown of concentration creasing her forehead, he knew that the problem was his alone. She seemed utterly happy—happier, even, than that slightly serious young girl he'd known all those years ago.

He, on the other hand, felt anything but relaxed. It didn't help that since they'd walked up to the terrace together their earlier conversation had been playing more or less on repeat inside his head.

Talking about his mother, remembering how devastated she had been by Paul's hurtful remarks and his lack of commitment, had made his muscles tense and a familiar feeling of anger and helplessness push against his ribcage.

For years those memories and feelings had been like fish in a pond over winter—there, but not there, still and silent beneath the ice. Now, though, it was as if he had smashed the frozen surface, and he couldn't seem to stop thinking about his mother and Paul. Himself and Margot.

He hadn't been consciously trying to rewrite history, and yet for the first time he could see that in so many ways his past had been driving his actions—pushing him to seek the certainty and legitimacy that his mother had craved. How else had he managed to build a global business worth billions in less than ten years?

His chest rose and fell.

Why else would he have proposed to Margot after seeing her in secret for just two months? And why else had he ignored logic and instinct and married her five days ago?

At the time, he'd justified his behaviour in any number of ways. Only he didn't care any more about the money he'd paid for the shares. Nor did he feel the need to take her business and turn it around, for he knew now that she hadn't judged him unworthy.

He breathed in sharply. Opening his eyes, he glanced over at where Margot was sitting, her sleek limbs gleaming in the sunlight. Always, right from the beginning, he'd seen their relationship from *his* point of view. It had been his past that mattered, his pride, his feelings—his motivation.

But this wasn't just about him.

'I had choices, and I walked into that chapel willingly.'

As her words replayed inside his head his thoughts slowed in time to his heartbeat, and suddenly and acutely he knew why he was feeling so uneasy.

Margot might be his wife, but the fact was there was no way she would have chosen to marry him if he hadn't forced the issue—forced her to choose between sacrificing herself or her family.

Really, what kind of a choice was that?

He had pushed her into this marriage, using the love she felt for her grandfather and her brother to get his own way. But now, having forced her to choose, where did that leave him— *them*?

'I was thinking about what you said earlier about doing other things.' Leaning forward, Max kissed Margot's bare shoulder. 'And I thought we might go scuba diving this morning. Danny can take us out in the boat, and we could spend a couple of hours in the water.'

They were eating lunch on the terrace. A delicate salad of lobster and asparagus, followed by tuna carpaccio and a lime tart.

Gazing up at him, Margot felt her skin grow warm, a pulse of love beating through her veins. 'I'd like that.'

She loved the serenity and the slow-motion way of life beneath the waves. There was something intensely peaceful about slipping beneath the surface of the water, and the deeper you went the easier it was to forget your land-locked worries.

And that was exactly what she needed to do—

what she had decided to do. Today she would concentrate on the good and stop dwelling on what she couldn't change. Most couples would envy the sexual connection that she and Max shared, and although he didn't love her he had confided in her, and that surely meant that he needed her for something other than sex.

It wasn't perfect, but few marriages were. And look how far they had come in just a few days.

She felt his fingers curl around hers.

'And you're okay swimming with sharks?' he asked softly.

She held his gaze. 'Isn't that what I've been doing all week?'

He grimaced. 'Is that how you see me?'

She studied his face. So much had changed in such a short time. A week ago she might only have noticed the ruthless line of his jaw, or the carefully guarded expression in his eyes. Now, though, she knew he was no shark. She'd experienced his softer side first-hand—not just when he was making love but in how he'd opened up to her.

'No, I don't think you're a shark.' Her eyes creased. 'You're more of a clownfish.'

There was a beat of silence, and then she shrieked with laughter as he grabbed her onto his lap and buried his face in the hollow of her neck.

She was still laughing when she heard a distant rumble. 'What was that?'

Turning, they both gazed towards the ocean. On the horizon, so far away it looked almost like smoke, a loose dark cloud was hovering above the sea. Down on the beach, the waves were slightly choppier and more uneven than usual.

'Must be a storm.' His arms tightened around her and he smiled down at her easily. 'Don't worry, it'll probably miss us. But even if it doesn't it won't last long at this time of year.' Picking up his cup, he took a gulp of coffee. 'I'll go talk to Danny. He tracks all the weather for miles, so he'll know if we can still go out and—'

He broke off as his mobile started to ring.

Glancing down at the screen, his face shifted, the smile fading. 'Sorry, it's my mother. I'd better take it.'

Before she had a chance to speak he was tipping her gently off his lap onto her chair and standing up and walking swiftly across the terrace to the pool, lifting the phone to his ear as he did so. Watching him, she felt oddly bereft, almost hurt by his leaving, for it felt as if he was rejecting her...

But it wasn't that, she told herself quickly. He just wasn't used to sharing that part of himself.

It was impossible to hear what he was saying, and she couldn't see the expression on his

face. But over the last few days she had become increasingly sensitive to the tiniest shift
in his manner and, staring at his broad back, she
knew something was wrong. His shoulders were
pressing against the flimsy fabric of his shirt as
though he was holding himself back—or holding something in.

She chewed her lip. Should she stay sitting
or should she go over to him? Or maybe she
shouldn't even be there.

She was just contemplating this new, third option when she heard Max hang up. For a moment she waited for him to turn round, her
heart bumping nervously against her ribs. But
he didn't turn round. He just carried on standing there in silence, his head slightly bowed as
though he was praying.

Suddenly she could bear it no longer. It was
probably a bad idea. Almost certainly it was.
Only she didn't know any other way to be, for
she cared that he was hurting. And so, standing
up, she walked towards him.

'Max—is everything okay?'

She breathed out softly. Around them the air
was heavy and motionless, and the birds were
suddenly unusually quiet, as though sensing the
sudden shift in tension on the terrace.

He turned slowly. 'Not really, no,' he said at last.

She felt cold on the inside. Trying not to think

the worst, she said quickly, 'Is something the matter with your mum?'

He nodded. 'She needs me to come home, so I'm going to have to go back to France.'

'To France?' Whatever answer she had been expecting, it wasn't that.

He stared at her impatiently. 'Yes—that's where she lives.'

'But why? What's happened?'

'It doesn't matter. You don't need to worry about it.'

His voice was curt, but it wasn't his voice that made a chill settle on her skin. Moments before he'd answered the phone his eyes had been soft and teasing. Now, though, they were hard and flat and distant. And just like that time reversed, so that suddenly he was back to being the same remote man who had confronted her in the boardroom.

'But I am worried,' she said simply. 'I can see you're upset—'

He looked over at her blankly, almost as though he wasn't quite sure who she was, and then, running a hand over his face, he sighed.

'She's got the press camped out on her doorstep. Somehow they've found out about us. There are hundreds of them, all waiting outside, trying to get photos and hassling the staff. I can't expect her to deal with that.'

'Of course not.' She moved swiftly to his side, her hand reaching for his. 'We can leave now.' She glanced down at her bikini. 'I'll just go and get changed—'

His fingers tightened on hers, but even if they had been standing on opposite sides of the pool she would have known that she'd said the wrong thing, for she felt his entire body tensing beside her.

'You don't have to do that,' he said curtly, and then, as though hearing the harshness in his own voice, he softened his refusal by lifting her hand to his mouth and kissing it. 'In fact, it's probably better if you don't. They want a story, and it will be far easier for me to give them one if I'm on my own. So just stay here. I will fix this, and then I'll fly back.'

'But—' Margot started to protest but it was too late. He had already let go of her hand and was walking purposefully towards the house.

She stared after him in silence, her body quivering with a mixture of confusion and frustration. Theoretically, she'd accepted that Max would never love her, but now, faced with concrete evidence of that fact, she felt angry and hurt.

She sort of understood why he didn't want her to go back with him. Max knew how to handle himself, and she certainly didn't enjoy dealing with the *paparazzi*. Nor did she want to meet his mother for the first time with a pack of howling press slavering outside for a photo. So perhaps it would be better if she stayed here.

But if that was true then why did she feel as though he was only telling her part of the story? And, more importantly, why was she still standing here when she should be asking him that question?

Striding into his dressing room, Max yanked down a shirt and pushed his arms into the sleeves. He grabbed a tie and knotted it round his neck, then pulled his jacket on. After so long in beachwear, he felt as if his clothes were as unfamiliar and unwieldy as a suit of armour. But he wasn't planning on wearing them for long, or staying in France for any more time than it took to get whatever legal decision he needed to protect his mother. However, he sure as hell wasn't going to make the trip in swim-shorts and flip-flops.

Or with Margot there.

Remembering the hurt expression on her face, he closed his eyes. He didn't want to leave her behind, but how could he take her with him? The press were relentless, and with a story like this they would be like the sharks he had jokingly mentioned over lunch. Hungry, ruthless and unstoppable.

Without her, he could handle them, and that was why he would be going back to France alone.

Gritting his teeth, he walked back into the bedroom and picked up his wallet and his watch. Frowning, he stared down at the face. If he left in the next hour he would be back sometime after—

'I want to come with you.'

He turned. Margot was standing in the doorway, not quite blocking it but with a stubborn set to her chin that suggested she might be about to do so.

He sighed. Had he really thought that she would just give up?

Holding her gaze, he shook his head. 'It's not a good idea. If we go together it will only turn into a feeding frenzy—and, frankly it's bad enough that they're hounding my mother. I don't need them turning on my wife as well.'

She stared at him mutinously. 'I disagree. If we both go back then we can give them what they want. The two of us together. Mr and Mrs Max Montigny.'

He glanced away from her. She was saying everything he'd ever wanted to hear, offering him the kind of support and loyalty that he had always craved, and yet...

Something shifted inside him—a tectonic

convergence of conversations and memories—
and he heard not just her words but the calm ac-
ceptance in the voice.

'I'm a fixer-upper. I make it all look perfect.'

His heart was beating fast and uneven, as
though he'd been running. Maybe because he
was running away from a truth that he didn't
want to face—away from facts that he could
never change, no matter how much he wanted to.

He took a deep breath, his gut tightening,
finally acknowledging the real reason why he
couldn't take her with him.

Margot had spent all her life fixing her family: managing her parents' marriage, her grandparents' expectations and the demands of her
brothers, sacrificing her plans and her hopes and
dreams time and time again.

And here, on this archipelago, he had made
her sacrifice herself to him. But knowing that,
was he really going to ask her to do it again?

He felt her eyes on his face, and then the touch
of her hand on his arm.

'I thought you wanted to be with me,' she said
softly. 'That's what you said.'

Watching his face grow still and remote, Margot felt a chill spread over her skin. He might
have spoken the words, but clearly he hadn't
meant them. Like so much of what Max said,

it bore little relation to what was going in that handsome head of his.

'I do—' he began.

Her pulse jumped and she took a step closer. 'So prove it. Take me with you. I should be there. I want to be there. I know it's been difficult between us, but I am your wife.'

Wife.

Remembering the vows they had taken, he felt suddenly unsteady, and a chill started to roll out over his skin. He had promised to love and to cherish her.

But he had lied.

Ever since the moment he had walked into the boardroom at the House of Duvernay headquarters he had treated her with a ruthlessness that now sickened him. A ruthlessness that equalled—no, *surpassed* Paul's treatment of his mother, for he had exploited her misfortune to give, by proxy, his mother the happy ending she'd so wanted.

It was all such a mess.

He'd made Margot a pawn—bullying her, blackmailing her, rushing her into marrying him. Using her to solve the issues inside his head in the same way that Paul had used his mother for sex and to boost his ego. Using the real love Margot felt for her family to get his own way. He had hurt her and humbled her, deliberately and repeatedly, and she had risen above his treatment in ways he could hardly fathom and certainly didn't deserve.

Any more than he deserved her support now.

What she *did* deserve, though, was to have the freedom to choose. To be with the person she wanted. Not be saddled with a life sentence to a man she had been to all intents and purposes forced to marry.

Margot stared at him, her frustration shifting up a gear. 'You wanted this, Max. You wanted this marriage. I thought you wanted—' Her insides turned over and abruptly she broke off, leaving the sentence unfinished.

He didn't want her.

She couldn't actually say the words out loud. Even thinking them was so painful that it hurt to breathe, but she knew she was right. The fact that he didn't want her to go with him told her everything she needed to know.

Had he trusted and valued her, then returning to France would have been the perfect opportunity for them to showcase their marriage in public. But he would rather go alone.

The thought ripped through her like a serrated knife.

Max stared down at her face. She had never looked more beautiful to him and he had never wanted her more. He felt a sudden warm rush of hope rising inside him. 'Okay, I'll take you with me,' he said slowly. 'But on one condition.'

He could feel the warmth fading, and in its place a chill spreading out as she looked up at him uncertainly.

'I want you to tell me the truth,' he said.

Outside the window he could see the darkening sky, feel the heaviness of the approaching storm, and yet it seemed feeble, even frivolous, compared to the tension swirling inside his chest.

'Okay.' She nodded, her brown eyes searching his face, her relief at his change of heart mingling with obvious apprehension at where the conversation was leading.

Holding her gaze, he cleared his throat. 'I want you to tell me why you agreed to marry me.'

Her face stilled, and she frowned. 'Well, because…'

She hesitated, and her eyes dropped as though she couldn't meet his gaze, and then he knew. He knew that it had all been worthless. He could never take Margot to meet his mother for she would know in an instant that it was a phony marriage. It would break her heart, and he could no more do that to her then continue to use guilt and financial threats to keep Margot as his wife.

Margot shivered. She wasn't sure what was

happening, just knew that they were no longer simply talking about whether or not she should return with him to France.

She tried again. 'You know why.'

'But I want you to tell me in your own words,' he said softly.

Too softly, she thought a moment later, her throat drying as she looked up into his taut, set face. 'I needed the money—' she began, but he cut her off.

'So there was no other reason.'

Yes, there was—there were. So many reasons—too many—but she wasn't brave enough to start listing them now.

It took her a moment to realise that he wasn't asking a question, just stating a fact. For perhaps a minute he stared at her in silence, and then, just as she was about to protest, to tell him that it wasn't that simple, he lowered his mouth to hers and kissed her gently.

Her heart lurched with relief, her fingers curling around the muscles of his arm as he deepened the kiss, her longing for him stealing her words, her thoughts, even her fear.

Reaching up, she clasped his face. But as she tried to deepen the kiss she felt his hands on hers, and suddenly he was stepping away from her, breathing unsteadily.

'Don't follow me,' he said, and the finality in

his voice cast a spell over her body, rooting her to the cold tiles.

She knew without asking that he didn't just mean out of the room. He meant to France, to wherever, and the shock knocked the air out of her lungs, so that before her stunned brain could even register what he was doing he had turned and walked swiftly out of the room.

CHAPTER TEN

IT TOOK THE first tiny clumps of raindrops slamming against the window to drag Margot's eyes away from the empty doorway. Hesitantly, as though she wasn't sure if her legs would respond, she took a step towards the bed and sank down onto it. Her body felt brittle, her breath leaden.

It hardly seemed possible, but Max had walked out on her. Not just out of the room, or even the villa, but out of her life. He hadn't actually said as much. But he hadn't needed to. She had seen it in his eyes. Something had happened between that phone call out on the terrace and her walking into the bedroom—some insight or decision that had turned him away from her, away from their marriage.

Curling her knees up to her chest, she hugged them against her body. Shock gave way to misery, and tears began sliding down over her cheeks, and then the shock returned and her heartbeat started to shake. Her body started shaking too, and she was glad suddenly that she was sitting down, for she knew that her legs were definitely not capable of holding her up, or of supporting the weight of misery in her chest.

She took a deep breath, striving for calm, but the pain in her chest was too loud, too demanding.

He'd left her. Max had left her.

After everything they'd been through, she'd thought for one brief, blissful moment that they had a chance, that maybe her love would be enough for the two of them to make their marriage work. But now it was all over before it had even got started.

She covered her mouth with her hand.

Was it really that surprising, though? The pull between them had only ever been sexual on his side, and what couple had ever managed to build a future on great sex?

Thinking about her parents' marriage, she felt her pulse quiver. Not a happy or healthy marriage, anyway.

Remembering his question, she felt her shoulders tighten. Would it have been any different if she'd told him the truth? That at first she'd told herself that she was marrying him for money, but that even then the real reason she'd agreed to his proposal was because she loved him, had never stopped loving him.

Love had been the reason she'd let him back

into her life. And the reason why she had agreed to turn her life upside down.

Only now he was gone, and the idea of his not being there was unimaginable. Agonising.

Suddenly she felt exhausted. Her eyes were blurry with tears again and her head was aching. But the pain would pass. Maybe not today, or tomorrow, or even in a year…or five. Sometime in the future, though, it would be just a dull ache above her heart, like the pain of losing her mother and her grandmother and Yves.

She had survived losing Max once, and she would do it again. But first she needed to sleep, for she was just so tired.

Crawling up towards the pillows, she pulled the sheet over her body and closed her eyes. Soothed by the steady, soporific sound of the rain striking the ground, she fell asleep.

It was the sound of the birds that woke her. Not right away. At first their cries were just background noise to the confused and unfinished dream she was having about Emile and Max and that boat she had seen on the second day of their honeymoon.

Opening her eyes, she gazed groggily around the room. It was still daylight and, grabbing her phone, she realised with shock that she had slept for nearly two hours. Judging by the fact that the sky was no longer dark, but streaked with palest pink and yellow, she had slept through the storm too. Outside, the surf sounded reassuringly soft and regular, and the air felt warm but fresh, as though it had just come out of a tumble drier.

She felt fresher too—less tired and less desperate, both her body and her mind revived by sleep. It wasn't that she felt any better about Max's rejection, just that she could see past it. Her heart might be in pieces, but that didn't mean her life had to be too. She had recovered from breaking up with him before, and the House of Duvernay had survived wars and recessions. It would survive Max Montigny.

Only somehow she didn't think that he was going to hang around anyway. He had walked out for a reason. Had the company been prosperous, then perhaps it might be different, but it was clear that he didn't want anything to do with her, and she felt sure that his feelings would extend to their business relationship.

Her mouth twisted. Obviously he would feel that way. To Max, all of this—including their marriage—had only ever been about business. She had been the one to start weaving fantasy through fact, letting the intimacy and intensity of the last few days sweep her away.

Perhaps for a short time it had swept him away too. Only when it had come to returning to reality, to leaving the perfect little self-contained bubble of their honeymoon, he'd come to his senses. And that was when he'd decided to walk.

Tears burned behind her eyes and she breathed out shakily. Even though accepting that fact felt like a knife being driven through her heart, in some ways she was glad of the pain, for it made her focus on herself in a way that she never had.

Before, there had always been a long list of people and problems: Colette, Emile, her grand-parents, Yves, Louis, Duvernay. And each time she had put her own life on hold in order to find a solution.

But from this moment on that was going to change. *She* had changed.

Her heart might be broken, but her brain was working just fine, and she knew that it was time to stop fixing other people's lives. Even though she wasn't quite sure how she was going to do it, she was going to start living *her* life—not the life decided by those around her.

A life on her own...without Max.

She might have wed in haste, like her parents, but that was where the similarity between their marriage and hers would end. Right now a life without Max felt like a life without warmth and sunlight, but however agonising it was to imagine, she was going to divorce him.

If she was going to make good on this promise to change then she needed her name and her business back. And that meant divorcing Max— although she would leave the details to the lawyers. She might have found the strength to deal with the concept theoretically, but it would be a long time before she would be willing or able to speak to him again—if ever.

First things first, though. She needed to go home.

She packed methodically, the rhythm of folding and layering her clothes helping her stay calm. Changing out of her bikini, she found a pair of skinny-fit jeans that she'd brought with her in case of a freakish cold spell, and a loose tobacco-coloured linen jumper. Her face was pale, and her eyes were slightly pink and swollen, and for a moment she wondered whether mascara and lipstick would make things better or worse. Deciding it would be easier just to wear dark glasses, she left her hair loose, picked up her bag and shoes and walked towards the door.

All that was left to do was thank the staff and make her way to the airport. But first she wanted one last walk along the beach.

Walking through the villa, she felt some of her self-control start to slip away, and suddenly she was fighting tears again. She had loved being here with Max, getting to know him, getting to know herself, but there was no point in thinking that way.

Swiping at her eyes, grateful that she hadn't bothered to apply mascara, she stepped out onto the terrace—and froze.

Max was sitting on the curved steps leading down to the pool. He was hunched over, his head in his hands, an empty glass lying on its side beside him.

She stared at him in stunned silence. What was he still doing here? Had the storm delayed his flight? And what exactly was she supposed to say to him now?

Glancing down, she felt her heartbeat skip erratically. He was still wearing the same charcoal-coloured suit, only it was soaking wet. She could see water dripping from the jacket, and the fabric was dark and swollen-looking. With shock, she realised that he must have been sitting out in the storm.

Carefully setting down her bag and shoes, she walked towards him. 'Max…?'

He looked up at her and she felt her heart twist, for his eyes were dull and colourless.

'I didn't know you were still here,' she said quietly.

He nodded. 'I couldn't leave.'

She bit her lip. 'Was it the storm?'

'The storm?' He frowned, as though he didn't understand her question.

'Did they close the airport?' Obviously they

had. What other reason would he have for still being here? Although she wasn't sure why he hadn't sheltered from the rain.

His eyes fixed on her face, and then slowly he shook his head. 'I didn't go the airport. I couldn't—'

His voice cracked and, glancing down at his hands, she saw that they were shaking. Suddenly she was shaking too.

Forcing herself to lift her chin, she said stiffly, 'Why not? Why couldn't you go?'

Her heart was beating so hard that she felt light-headed. It didn't mean anything, him being here. There was probably some logical and simple reason. But—

She drew a breath, trying to calm herself.

Why else would he still be at the villa?

Don't even go there, she thought desperately.

But she couldn't help herself. From the moment she had walked out onto the terrace and seen him it had been there, hidden beneath the surface but still there, a longing and a hope that she knew was stupid and senseless. And yet she couldn't stop herself from feeling it.

'I couldn't leave you,' he said slowly.

She stared at him mutely, not daring to ask any of the questions milling around inside her head, not willing to have her hopes crushed again.

Suddenly she knew that she couldn't stay standing up. With legs that shook slightly, she sat down beside him. Up close, she could see that his shirt was drier than his suit, but still damp. She felt her throat swell.

Reaching over, she carefully righted the glass. 'Did you stay out here in the storm?'

Max shrugged, then nodded. 'I tried to leave, but I just couldn't.'

'What about your mother?'

Hearing the concern in her voice, he flinched inwardly. Even now she was thinking about someone other than herself.

'My lawyers got an emergency injunction so the photographers can't go within fifty metres of her house, so she's doing okay.'

He watched the tension in her beautiful face ease a little, and then she reached out and touched his jacket.

'And what about you? You're soaked through. Why didn't you come inside?'

For a moment he couldn't speak past the ache in his throat. And then he said, 'Because I knew if I saw you that I'd never be able to do it. I'd never be able to leave you. And I have to leave, Margot. I can't do this to you any more.' Clenching his jaw, he breathed out unsteadily.

'Do what?' Her brown eyes were searching his.

'All of this. Everything. I've treated you so badly, and I don't want to *be* that person.' He ran a hand over his face, suddenly struggling for words. 'I don't want to hurt you.'

Margot felt suddenly close to tears. 'So why are you leaving me, then?' She stared at him, frustration overriding her fear. 'If you don't want to hurt me then why are you doing this?'

He hesitated, his expression stricken. 'You did all this to protect your family. You're such a good person, Margot. And I'm not. You deserve better than me.'

Her chest tightened. 'Max—'

He shook his head. 'I want to be with you. That's all I want—all I've ever wanted.' His mouth twisted. 'That's why I came back to France. Why I bought the shares. Why I offered to marry you. For a long time I didn't want to admit it to myself, let alone you, but I need you to understand why we can't be together.'

Margot couldn't look at him. 'And why *is* that, Max?' Her voice split, the hurt and the longing rising to the surface. 'Why can't we be together?'

His hand slid over hers, and reluctantly she turned to face him.

'Because I love you,' he said softly. 'But I know you don't love me. I know you only married me because you love your family, and I'm sorry for making you do that. Sorry for everything else I've done and said.'

She gazed at him, feeling hot and dazed, as

though she'd been sitting in the sun all morning, too stunned with shock and happiness to speak.

'You love me?' she croaked.

He nodded, his fingers tightening around hers.

'And what about if I love you?' she said shakily.

He stared down into her face. 'But you don't, do you?'

She couldn't reply, but she knew that she must be nodding, and smiling, because suddenly he breathed out raggedly and then he was pulling her onto his lap, wrapping his arms around her, holding her close, then closer still, as though he never wanted to let her go.

'You're such an idiot,' she whispered. 'Of *course* I love you, Max. I've loved you since I was nineteen years old.'

Lifting her face, she saw that his face was damp now too—but with tears, not rain.

'It nearly broke me, losing you,' he said, and his voice was hoarse with the emotions he was no longer trying to hide. 'I need you like I need air and water and food. Without you, nothing matters. Without you, I have nothing. I *am* nothing.'

Searching his face, she knew that he was telling the truth. 'Not to me,' she said softly. 'You're my husband, and my heart belongs to you.' She smiled up at him. 'And now I think we should get you out of that suit.'

He gazed down at her, his eyes gleaming in the sunlight, and she felt a rush of pure love for him as his mouth curved upwards.

'That has to be your most transparent attempt yet to get my clothes off.'

Reaching up, she curled her arm around his neck. 'Did it work?'

In answer to her question he scooped her into his arms and stood up, the burn of his gaze melting her bones and searing her skin.

'I think so. But you know I never like to leave anything to chance. So let's go and make certain.'

And, turning, he carried her back into the villa.

* * * * *

If you enjoyed
Revenge at the Altar,
*you'll love these other stories
by Louise Fuller!*

Claiming His Wedding Night
Blackmailed Down the Aisle
Kidnapped for the Tycoon's Baby
Surrender to the Ruthless Billionaire

Available now!